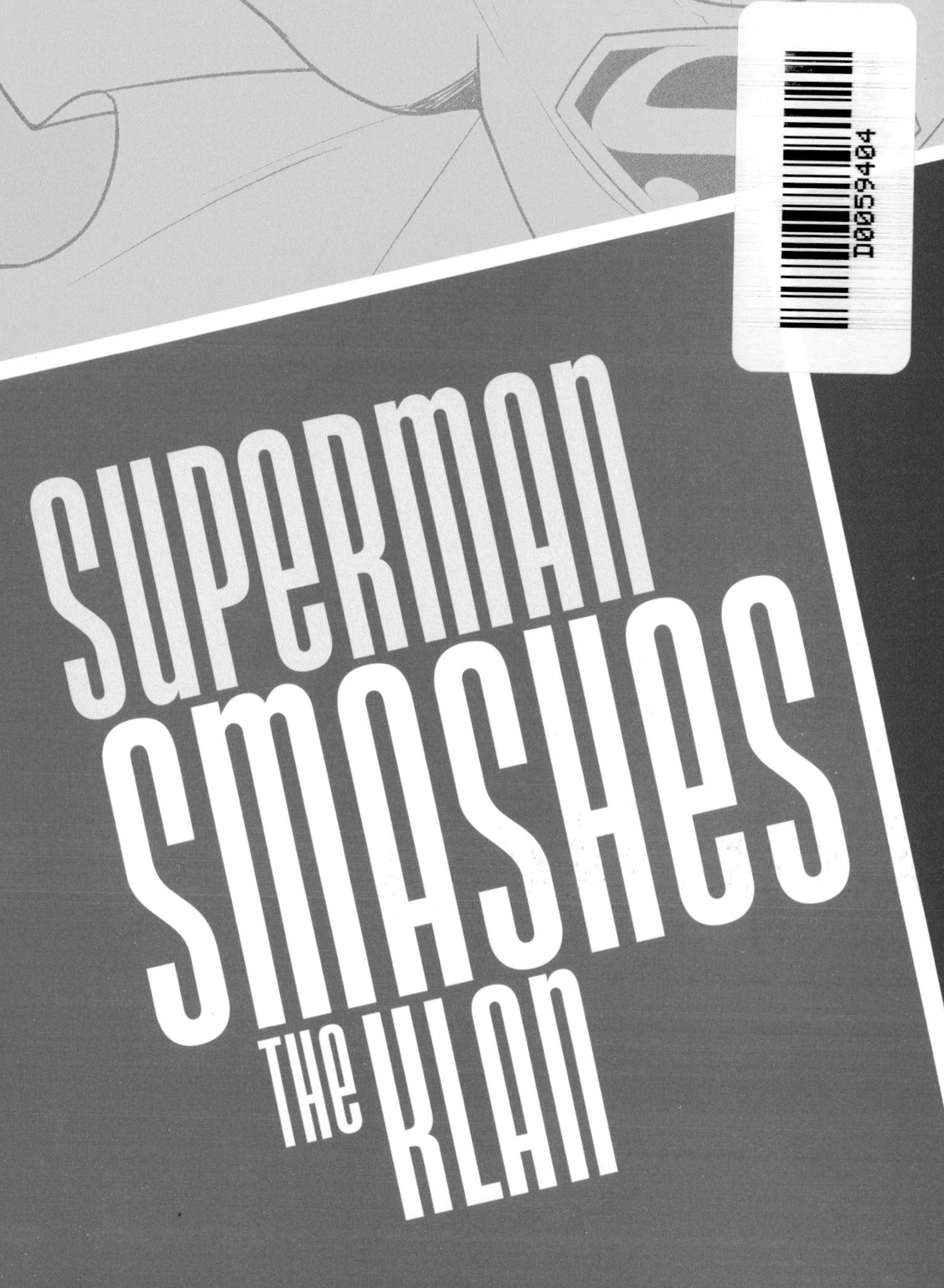
SUPERMAN
SMASHES
THE KLAN

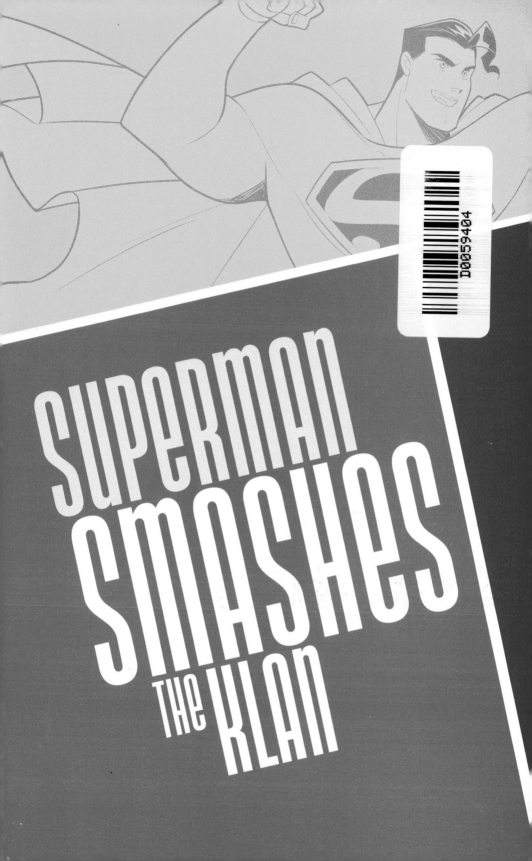

SUPERMAN SMASHES THE KLAN

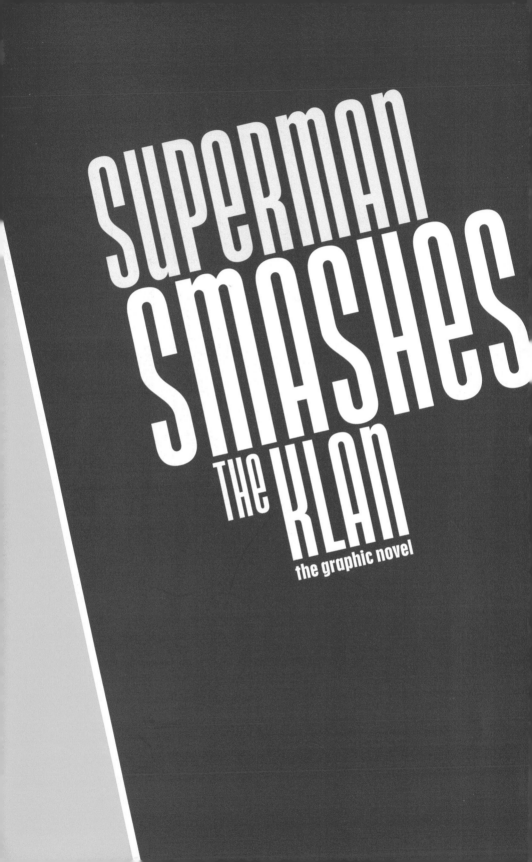

the graphic novel

written by **GENE LUEN YANG**

art by **GURIHIRU**

lettering by **JANICE CHIANG**

Superman created by Jerry Siegel and Joe Shuster. By special arrangement with the Jerry Siegel family.

SUPERMAN SMASHES THE KLAN

DC Comics, 2900 West Alameda Ave., Burbank, CA 91505
Printed by LSC Communications, Crawfordsville, IN, USA
4/3/20
First Printing
ISBN: 978-1-77950-421-0

PEFC Certified
This product is from sustainably managed forests and controlled sources
PEFC
PEFC/29-31-337
www.pefc.org

Library of Congress Cataloging-in-Publication Data

Names: Yang, Gene Luen, author. | Chiang, Janice, letterer. | Gurihiru, artist.
Title: Superman smashes the Klan : the graphic novel / written by Gene Luen Yang ; art illustrations by Gurihiru ; lettering by Janice Chiang.
Description: Burbank : DC Comics, [2020] | "Superman created by Jerry Siegel and Joe Shuster, by special arrangement with the Jerry Siegel family" | Includes bibliographical references. | Audience: Ages 13+ | Audience: Grades 10-12 | Summary: When Dr. Lee moves his family to Metropolis, his son Tommy adjusts to the new neighborhood while daugher Roberta feels out of place, so when the evil Klan of the Fiery Cross begins a string of terrorist attacks on the city, Superman fights them, and Roberta and Superman soon learn to embrace their own unique features that set them apart.
Identifiers: LCCN 2020010185 (print) | LCCN 2020010186 (ebook) | ISBN 9781779504210 (paperback) | ISBN 9781779504227 (ebook)
Subjects: LCSH: Graphic novels. | CYAC: Graphic novels. | Superman (Fictitious character)--Fiction. | Justice--Fiction. | Identity--Fiction.
nt) | LCC PZ7.7.Y35 (ebook) |

For kids everywhere.
—Gene and Gurihiru

Including my own.
—Gene

CHAPTER 1

THE METROPOLIS DAM. 1946.
TREMBLE, AMERICAN SCUM!
TREMBLE BEFORE THE MIGHT OF THE ATOM MAN, AVENGER OF THE MASTER RACE!
BKAM!
EXCUSE ME, MR. ATOM MAN? LOIS LANE, DAILY PLANET. THIS IS MY ASSOCIATE JIMMY OLSEN.
HIYA!
I'VE GOT A FEW QUESTIONS FOR YOU, IF YOU DON'T MIND.
B-BUT THE ATOM MAN DOES MIND! THE ATOM MAN MINDS VERY MUCH!
GREAT. FIRST QUESTION: WHAT ARE YOU HOPING TO ACCOMPLISH BY BUSTING A HOLE IN THE METROPOLIS DAM?
REVENGE! YOU AMERICAN SCUM HUMILIATED THE MASTER RACE! NOW, THE ATOM MAN WILL—
REVENGE. GOT IT. SECOND QUESTION: HAVE YOU ACTUALLY THOUGHT THIS THROUGH?
I GUESS WHAT I'M REALLY ASKING IS—
HAVEN'T YOU HEARD OF METROPOLIS' MOST FAMOUS CITIZEN?
SNAP!
GOOD OL' LOIS AND JIMMY—

—SO FEARLESS. HONESTLY, I FIND THEM INSPIRING.
GASP!
THE SUPERMAN!
NO "THE." THE "THE" IS A BIT PRETENTIOUS, DON'T YOU THINK?
HEYYY! SO YOU HAVE HEARD OF HIM!
SNAP!

OOF!
POW!
IT'S JUST "SUPERMAN," PLEASE.
THE ATOM MAN DOES NOT FEAR THE SO-CALLED SUPER-STRENGTH OF THE SUPERMAN!
YOU SEE, THIS MASTERFULLY ENGINEERED DEVICE PUMPS SUPER-SUPER-STRENGTH INTO THE ATOM MAN'S HEART!

NAZI SCIENCE MADE THE ATOM MAN VERY MUCH STRONGER THAN THE SUPERMAN! HA HA!
POW!
HM. IMPRESSIVE RIGHT HOOK.
BUT "VERY MUCH STRONGER"...
BAM!
BAM!
BAM!
IS PUSHING IT...
DON'T YOU THINK?
NGH...
THE ATOM MAN PROMISES THAT WHEN THE ATOM MAN NEXT RETURNS—
Click!
—THE SUPERMAN SHALL TREMBLE BEFORE THE MIGHT OF THE ATOM MAN!
FWOOOM!
LEAP, SUPERMAN, LEAP! HE'S GETTING AWAY!
HE'S NOT GONNA LEAP. HE'S GONNA KNOCK HIM OUT OF THE SKY.

WHY WAIT, ATOM MAN?!
WHY NOT MAKE ME TREMBLE RIGHT NOW?!
KRUNK!
FSSSS!
MS. LANE, HOW'D YOU KNOW—?
IT'S MY JOB TO KNOW. SUPERMAN'S FASTER THAN A SPEEDING BULLET—
KRASH!
"—MORE POWERFUL THAN A LOCOMOTIVE, ABLE TO LEAP TALL BUILDINGS IN A SINGLE BOUND!"
I'VE READ YOUR ARTICLE MANY, MANY TIMES.
THEN YOU KNOW THAT EVEN SUPERMAN HAS HIS LIMITS. THE HIGHEST HE'S EVER LEAPT IS TWENTY STORIES. IT'S NOT LIKE HE CAN FLY.
THE ATOM MAN WAS OUT OF RANGE.
WEEEOOO! WEEEOOO!
LET'S SEE ABOUT TURNING OFF THAT "MASTERFULLY ENGINEERED DEVICE"!
HNN...
IT'S THE SMELL THAT HITS ME FIRST.
LIKE ASH AND ROT AND...SOMETHING ELSE. SOMETHING SO FAMILIAR IT BRINGS TEARS TO MY EYES.
YET FOR THE LIFE OF ME, I CAN'T REMEMBER WHAT IT IS.

THE SMELL FIRST, THEN THE PAIN.
FOR AS LONG AS I CAN REMEMBER, I'VE PRETENDED. WHENEVER SOMEBODY ACCIDENTALLY BUMPED INTO ME OR STEPPED ON MY TOE, I'VE HAD TO FAKE A WINCE. BUT THIS...
THIS IS REAL.
IF THAT WEIRD GREEN CRYSTAL CAN AFFECT EVEN ME, IT'LL KILL THE OTHERS.
LOIS... JIMMY... STAY BACK...!
OH NO... WHAT HAPPENED TO MY HAND?!
SUPERMAN...?
THE DEVICE ON ATOM MAN'S CHEST... THE SOURCE OF HIS POWER... IT'S...

—IT'S NO LONGER A CONCERN.
INSPECTOR HENDERSON...!
RIIIP!
WILL YOU LOOK AT THAT! WITHOUT HIS FANCY GADGET, HE'S JUST A SCRAWNY KID!
THE ATOM MAN...IS DONE FOR...

YOU SAVING THAT LID FOR A SOUVENIR, SUPERMAN?
NO... HERE YOU GO...
IS HE JUST TOO POLITE TO SAY ANYTHING ABOUT MY HAND?

YOU DON'T LOOK SO GOOD... YOU'RE NOT COMING DOWN WITH A COLD, ARE YOU? I DIDN'T KNOW THAT WAS EVEN POSSIBLE!
I'M...OKAY, INSPECTOR.
SNAP
NOW THAT THE GREEN CRYSTAL IS SEALED UP AGAIN, MY HAND IS BACK TO NORMAL! THE PAIN IS GONE, TOO...BUT I CAN STILL SMELL THE SMELL.

CHICKEN SOUP, BIG GUY. SOUP WILL MAKE YOU SUPER AGAIN IN NO TIME.
GET IT? "SOUP-ER"? HA HA!
I'D BE HAPPY TO BRING OVER A POT FOR YOU, SUPERMAN.
IN EXCHANGE FOR SOME ANSWERS.

MY CHICKEN SOUP OFFER STILL STANDS!

I THOUGHT YOU SAID YOU'RE A TERRIBLE COOK!

SNAP!

JIMMY! GOOD TO SEE YOU!

RIGHT BACK ATCHA, SUPERMAN!

I PUT ON MY BEST SMILE AS I LEAVE. NO SENSE WORRYING LOIS OR JIMMY.

*NO MATTER HOW FAST I RUN, THOUGH, I CAN'T GET AWAY FROM THAT **SMELL**.*

*I THINK I'M GOING TO BE **SICK**.*

I THINK I'M GOING TO BE SICK.
UGH...
I'M NOT SURE IF IT'S THE WAY THE CAR IS MOVING OR THE FACT THAT WE JUST LEFT THE ONLY HOME I'VE EVER KNOWN. MAYBE BOTH.

LAN-SHIN, ARE YOU NOT FEELING WELL?
MA CAME TO AMERICA A FEW MONTHS BEFORE MARRYING DAD. SHE'S STILL MOST COMFORTABLE SPEAKING CANTONESE.
IN ENGLISH, DEAR.

YES...YOU RIGHT. I FORGET. LAN-SHIN, YOU YOU...
INCLUDING OUR NAMES.

ROBERTA, YOU...BAD TUMMY?

THE CAR IS MAKING MY STOMACH A BIT GURGLY, IS ALL.
AW, WHY DO YOU ALWAYS GOTTA BE SUCH A POOPER, ROBERTA?
THIS IS WAY MORE FUN THAN THE BUS!

YES, TOMMY. I'M PURPOSELY MAKING MY STOMACH GURGLY JUST TO RUIN YOUR FUN.
PERHAPS YOU'LL FEEL BETTER IF YOU LOOK OUT THE WINDOW.

WHOAAA.
CAN YOU BELIEVE WE GET TO LIVE IN METROPOLIS, SIS?
WE'VE LIVED IN METROPOLIS OUR WHOLE LIVES, DUMMY!
HEY! WHO'RE YOU CALLING A DUMMY?!
WHO'RE YOU CALLING A POOPER?!
CHILDREN! SETTLE DOWN!
AND TOMMY IS RIGHT. WE LIVED IN CHINATOWN. IT'S NOT THE SAME. YOU'LL SEE.

THE DAILY PLANET BUILDING LOOKS LIKE IT'S STRAIGHT OUTTA THE FUTURE! HOW DOES THAT NOT MAKE YOU FEEL BETTER, SIS?
BLARF!

IT'S STILL THERE, EVEN AFTER I CHANGED OUT OF MY SUPERMAN UNIFORM. I CAN'T SEEM TO SHAKE THE SMELL OF THAT GREEN CRYSTAL.
SNIFF
SNIFF

I BROUGHT YOU COFFEE, CLARK.
LOIS! HI! TH-THANKS!
WHERE WERE YOU THIS MORNING?
I HAD TO TAKE CARE OF A, UM...AN ERRAND BEFORE COMING IN TO WORK.

WELL, YOU MISSED OUT ON A TREMENDOUS STORY. AGAIN.
I HAD TO TAKE JIMMY WITH ME INSTEAD. AGAIN.
LANE! YOU'VE REALLY DONE IT THIS TIME!

SUPERMAN VERSUS A NAZI CREEP WHO NEVER GOT THE MEMO THAT WE WON THE WAR?! OH, BE STILL MY HEART!
TREMENDOUS WORK, LANE!
THANK YOU, PERRY.
SEE, CLARK? TREMENDOUS.

UH... KENT? WHY IN *TARNATION* ARE YOU SNIFFING YOURSELF LIKE THAT?
OH! *UM...*
DO LAUNDRY ONCE IN A WHILE AND YOU WON'T HAVE THAT PROBLEM.

HEH HEH! APPRECIATE THE *ADVICE*, LOIS!
WELP, BACK TO WORK FOR ME! I'LL CATCH YOU TWO LATER!
WAIT, WHERE ARE YOU GOING?! THIS IS *YOUR* OFFICE!

HOW IS *THAT GUY* ONE OF MY BEST REPORTERS?
I ASK MYSELF THAT EVERY DAY.

SPLASH

COME ON, CLARK. GET IT TOGETHER.

AAAH!
HOW...?
WEEEOOOO! WEEEOOOO!
A POLICE SIREN IN THE DISTANCE. FIVE MILES AWAY, TOPS.
PA ALWAYS SAID, MINDING YOURSELF TOO MUCH IS A GOOD WAY TO LOSE YOUR MIND.
TIME FOR ME TO MIND SOMEONE ELSE.

EEEW. I GOT THROW-UP ALL OVER MY JACKET. AND MY HANDS.
THIS JACKET'S GOTTEN TOO SMALL FOR YOU, ANYWAY. I'LL SEW YOU A NEW ONE AS SOON AS I CAN.
NO, NO. WE CAN AFFORD TO BUY HER A NEW JACKET NOW.
AND LET'S SPEAK ENGLISH, DEAR.
DAD! NO! LET ME KEEP IT FOR NOW, AT LEAST! PLEEEASE!
I'LL PICK ONE UP AT THE DEPARTMENT STORE THAT DOESN'T LOOK SO... ANTIQUATED. YOU'LL LOVE IT, ROBERTA. YOU'LL SEE.
I'VE WORN THAT JACKET EVERY DAY FOR THE LAST TWO YEARS, EVEN IN THE MIDDLE OF SUMMER.
WITHOUT IT, I'M ALL NERVES. A REAL WEIRDO.
GOODNESS, MY NEW BOSS AND COLLEAGUE HAVE COME TO VISIT! WHERE'S TOMMY?!
INSIDE UNPACKING, I THINK.
THEN IT'S UP TO YOU, ROBERTA! I EXPECT IMPECCABLE MANNERS!
WELCOME TO THE GREAT CITY OF METROPOLIS, LEES!
FAMILY, MAY I INTRODUCE DR. SEGRET WILSON AND DR. WILLIAM JENNINGS!
YOU MUST BE YOUNG ROBERTA! PLEASURE TO MAKE YOUR—
NO—NO HANDSHAKE—THROW-UP!
ROBERTA!
SEE WHAT I MEAN? WEIRDO.

WOW...WILL YOU LOOK AT THIS HOUSE! IT'S NICER THAN *MINE!*

SOME GUYS HAVE ALL THE *LUCK.* MUST BE NICE, EH, LEE?

IS THAT A BIRD...?
NO, A PLANE.
A PAPER AIRPLANE.
MY BROTHER AND I HAVE BEEN PULLING THIS SAME TRICK SINCE WE WERE LITTLE.
Sorry for calling you a pooper. Can we be friends again?
( ) Yes
( ) No
SIGH.
IT WORKS EVERY TIME.
HERE, TOMMY.

Sorry about calling you a pooper. Can we be friends again?
(X) Yes I am sorry too.
( ) You are often not a dummy.

I'M FEELING GENEROUS, SIS, SO I'LL LET YOU CHOOSE. TOP BUNK OR BOTTOM?
I'LL TAKE THE BOTTOM.

IF YOU INSIST!
I KNEW HE WANTED THE TOP.

Y'KNOW, THE VIEW UP HERE IS SOMETHING ELSE!

GOSH... IS THAT... IT'S GOTTA BE! AND HE'S COMING OUR WAY!
QUICK, ROBERTA! OUTSIDE!

WHOAAA.

WHOOOSH!

WAS THAT... *SUPERMAN?*

SURE WAS! HE RUNS ACROSS *TELEPHONE WIRES* SO HE WON'T GET IN THE WAY OF TRAFFIC.

WELCOME TO THE NEIGHBORHOOD! THE NAME'S *JIMMY OLSEN.* I'M YOUR ACROSS-THE-STREET NEIGHBOR!

HEY, JIMMY! I'M *TOMMY LEE.*

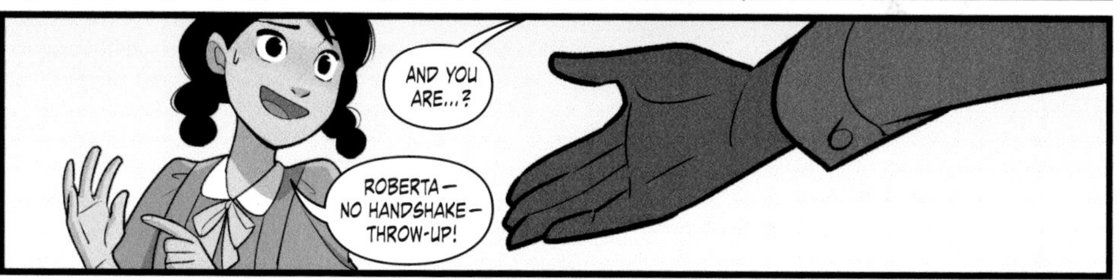

SWIIING!
MISS!
PAFF!
STRIIIKE THREE!
TURNS OUT *THE UNITY HOUSE* IS A COMMUNITY CENTER STARTED BY—AND THIS SOUNDS LIKE THE SETUP FOR A JOKE, BUT IT'S NOT—A PRIEST, A MINISTER, AND A RABBI.
HOLYYY—!
THAT LEE KID'S GOT A *ROCKET* FOR AN ARM!
YOU SAID IT, FATHER SHAIN. HOLYYY.

JACKET OR NO, YOU CAN DO THIS, ROBERTA. YOU CAN MAKE FRIENDS.
YOU WASHED YOUR HANDS AND EVERYTHING.
THEY WANTED TO BRING THE YOUNG PEOPLE OF METROPOLIS TOGETHER.
EVEN THE WEIRDOS.

HI. I'M ROBERTA LEE.
I WASHED MY HANDS.
UM? THAT'S VERY, UH...CLEAN OF YOU.

WAIT...THE PITCHER MUST BE YOUR BROTHER! ARE YOU CHINESE OR JAPANESE?
CHINESE.
OH, THANK GOODNESS! Y'KNOW, I'VE NEVER MET A CHINESE BEFORE! UP CLOSE LIKE THIS, I MEAN!

YOUR BROTHER'S SPECTACULAR! YOU THINK IT'D BE OKAY IF I GO SAY HELLO? HOW DO YOU SAY HELLO IN CHINESE?
NEIH HOU.
BUT WE SPEAK ENGLISH, TOO.
OBVIOUSLY.
IS THIS WHAT MY LIFE WILL BE LIKE FROM NOW ON? ALWAYS WATCHING FROM THE SIDELINES?
SIGH.
I MISS MY JACKET.
I MISS HOME.

—JUST SPECTACULAR!
AW, IT WAS NOTHIN'!

A ROCKET FOR AN ARM, I TELL YOU!

PERHAPS WE SHOULD—
WAY AHEAD OF YOU, RABBI STONE!
HEY, TOMMY! I GOT SOMETHING FOR YOU!

WILL YA LOOK AT THAT! THE CAP'S A PERFECT FIT! HOW WOULD YOU LIKE TO JOIN THE UNITY HOUSE BASEBALL TEAM?
ARE YOU SERIOUS?
ATTABOY, TOMMY!

HEY, NEW KID! HOW ABOUT YOU SHOW ME WHATCHA GOT?!
NOW, HOLD ON A SECOND, CHUCK! THAT'S NO WAY TO TALK TO YOUR NEW TEAMMATE!

WHO'S THAT?
CHUCK RIGGS, OUR STARTING PITCHER. OR HE WAS, AT LEAST, BEFORE YOU CAME ALONG.

MY NAME'S TOMMY, NOT "NEW KID"! AND I'LL BE HAPPY TO SHOW YOU WHAT I GOT AS SOON AS YOU STOP CROWDING THE PLATE!
BAH! JUST PITCH!
STEP BACK! I'M AFRAID I MIGHT BEAN YOU!
LISTEN TO HIM, CHUCK! GET BACK!
AW! YOU'RE AFRAID?!
PITCH, YA YELLOW BANANA!
FINE.

SMACK!
OW!
CHUCK!
CRIPES!
WHAT KIND OF KID WEARS BOOTS TO BASEBALL PRACTICE?
CHUCK! ARE YOU ALL RIGHT?!
HNN...
I'M SO SORRY! CAN I HELP YOU UP, BUDDY?
I'M NOT YOUR "BUDDY," CHINA BOY!

MR. RIGGS! WATCH YOUR WORDS!
YOU SAW WHAT HAPPENED, REVEREND LEEDS! THAT CHINA—
THAT CHINESE KID BEANED ME!
HEY, I TOLD YOU TO STEP BACK!
IT WAS AN ACCIDENT, CHUCK! AND HE APOLOGIZED! AS MANAGER OF THIS TEAM, I'M GONNA ASK YOU TO APOLOGIZE TO TOMMY FOR CALLING HIM NAMES!
I'M NOT APOLOGIZING! NOT TO THE LIKES OF HIM!
THEN I'M SORRY, CHUCK.
YOU'RE FIRED.
YOU KIDDING ME, OLSEN?! WE GOT THE CHAMPIONSHIP COMING UP! YOU'RE REALLY GONNA CHOOSE THIS...THIS CHING-CHONG OVER ME?
CALL ME THAT AGAIN, I DARE YOU!
GUYS, GUYS! STOP!

CHUCK— NO FIGHTING— COWARD!
HA! THERE'S A CHINA GIRL, TOO?
A CHINA GIRL WHO BARELY SPEAKS ENGLISH.
I FOCUS ON WHAT I HAVE TO DO TO PROTECT TOMMY.
...
I SPEAK ENGLISH JUST FINE.
WHAT I'M ASKING IS, ARE YOU THE KIND OF COWARD WHO'S WILLING TO FIGHT A GIRL HALF YOUR SIZE?
BECAUSE THAT'S WHAT YOU'LL HAVE TO DO TO GET TO HIM.
HERE, CHINA GIRL.
MAYBE OLSEN'LL INVITE YOU ON THE TEAM, TOO.
COME ON, EVERYBODY! FORGET THAT SOREHEAD! WE GOT A PRACTICE TO RUN!

LATER...
CHUCK! CHUCK RIGGS!
YOUR MOTHER PAID GOOD MONEY FOR THIS JERSEY! WHY'S IT IN THE TRASH?!
I...I GOT FIRED FROM THE TEAM, UNCLE MATT.
A KID ACCIDENTALLY BEANED ME AND I LOST MY TEMPER. YOU'RE ALWAYS TELLING ME NOT TO LOSE MY TEMPER.
THAT'S RIGHT. A MAN'S CHARACTER IS ROOTED IN HIS SELF-CONTROL.
YOU'LL GO BACK AND APOLOGIZE TOMORROW. IT WILL BE GOOD FOR BOTH YOU AND THE TEAM. THEY'RE GOING TO NEED THEIR STARTING PITCHER.
OH, I DON'T KNOW ABOUT THAT. THE NEW KID, THE ONE WHO BEANED ME, HAS A GREAT FASTBALL. OLSEN PROBABLY GAVE HIM MY SPOT.
WHAT?! LET ME GUESS: THIS KID'S NAME IS KOWALSKI OR O'MALLEY OR SOMETHING-STEIN!
HIS NAME IS TOMMY LEE.
"LEE"...I HEARD ABOUT THAT FAMILY! HIS FATHER MUST BE THE ONE WHO TOOK THE JOB AT THE HEALTH DEPARTMENT!
SO THIS LEE KID BEANS YOU, THEN REPLACES YOU? ABSOLUTELY DEVIOUS.
FIRST THE POLICE DEPARTMENT, NOW THE HEALTH DEPARTMENT AND EVEN A KIDS' BASEBALL TEAM... WHAT IS THIS CITY COMING TO?
I DON'T KNOW IF HE MEANT IT LIKE THAT, UNCLE MATT...
OH, DON'T BE NAIVE, CHUCK! HIS KIND ARE DEVIOUS BY NATURE!
I'M TAKING YOU TO A MEETING TONIGHT. WE'RE GOING TO MAKE SURE THAT FOLKS LIKE YOU AND ME AREN'T REPLACED EVER AGAIN!

WHAT ARE YOU SO SORE ABOUT?!
I DON'T NEED MY LITTLE SISTER DEFENDING ME, ROBERTA! THAT WAS HUMILIATING!
TOMMY, YOU JUST STARTED MAKING FRIENDS HERE! YOU JUST GOT YOURSELF A BRAND-NEW BASEBALL CAP!
AND YOU WERE JUST GONNA SOCK THAT JERK IN FRONT OF JIMMY AND THOSE OTHER KIDS AND THOSE HOLY-ROLLERS?! WHAT DO YOU THINK WOULD'VE HAPPENED THEN?!
THAT JERK WOULD'VE THOUGHT TWICE BEFORE CALLING ME NAMES NEXT TIME!
NO, YOU DUMMY! YOU WOULD'VE HAD TO GIVE BACK YOUR STUPID BASEBALL CAP, THAT'S WHAT!
FITTING IN COMES SO EASILY TO YOU, YOU'VE NEVER EVEN THOUGHT ABOUT HOW YOU ACTUALLY DO IT!
...
ROBERTA! WAIT!
YOU SEE THE WAY CHUCK LOOKED AT YOU WHEN YOU STOOD UP TO HIM?
TALK ABOUT A DUMMY. HA HA!

THIS IS AN *HISTORIC EVENT*, CHUCK.

THE FIRST OF ITS KIND HERE IN *METROPOLIS*.

UNCLE MATT, WHAT—?

WHEN I AM IN UNIFORM, YOU WILL ADDRESS ME AS THE *GRAND SCORPION*.

TAKE YOURS FROM THE BOX, THOUGH YOU'RE NOT TO WEAR IT UNTIL AFTER WE COMPLETE THE *INITIATION CEREMONY*.

B-BUT, UNCLE— I MEAN, *GRAND SCORPION*, WHY ARE WE HERE?! I-I READ ABOUT THIS AT SCHOOL...ISN'T THIS A GROUP OF HATEFUL *BIGOTS?!*

LIES PERPETUATED BY *CORRUPT* NEWSPAPERS AND TEXTBOOKS! WE DON'T *HATE* ANYONE, CHUCK!

ONE RACE! ONE COLOR! ONE RELIGION!
THAT IS THE MISSION OF THE KLAN OF THE FIERY KROSS...
TO BURN AWAY AMERICA'S IMPURITIES!

IT'S GOTTEN **WORSE.**
MY ENTIRE APARTMENT IS NOW FILLED WITH THAT SMELL.

BUT HOW CAN THAT BE? THE **GREEN CRYSTAL** IS SAFELY IN THE HANDS OF THE METROPOLIS POLICE DEPARTMENT.

IT'S ALL IN MY HEAD. IT **HAS** TO BE.

MAYBE I **AM** COMING DOWN WITH SOMETHING. I BET I CAN FIND A CAN OF **CHICKEN SOUP** IN THE KITCHEN CUPBOARD.

BRBL...
BRBL...
BRBL...

?!

SOMEONE'S BROKEN IN!

IT'LL BE TOO OBVIOUS IF I CHANGE INTO UNIFORM NOW. I'LL HAVE TO CONFRONT THEM AS **CLARK.**

BRBL...
BRBL...
BRBL...

MA...?

PA...?

?!

THIS IS A *DREAM*, RIGHT? YOU'RE A *DREAM*!

THEIR VOICES...

I'VE HEARD THEIR VOICES *BEFORE*.
SMALLVILLE. 1926.
CLARK! COME LOOK AT THIS!
WHAT IS IT, PA?
I'VE BEEN TINKERING WITH IT FOR MONTHS AND MONTHS!

CAN'T SAY FOR SURE, BUT I THINK IT'S SOME SORT OF RECORDING DEVICE, LIKE A PHONOGRAPH. **LISTEN.**
Click

SOUNDS LIKE PEOPLE TALKING IN SOME OTHER LANGUAGE! WHERE'D YOU GET IT?
IT WAS WITH YOU WHEN WE FOUND YOU, SON.
JONATHAN, DEAR? MIGHT I HAVE A WORD?

WHAT ARE YOU DOING?!
HE'S BEEN ***ASKING*** QUESTIONS EVER SINCE HE FIGURED OUT HE'S ***ADOPTED.*** DON'T YOU WANT HIM TO HAVE ***ANSWERS?***
EVENTUALLY, I SUPPOSE, BUT NOT YET!

MARTHA, OUR SON IS ***EXTRAORDINARY.*** AND HE DESERVES TO KNOW ***JUST*** HOW EXTRAORDINARY!
OF COURSE HE'S EXTRAORDINARY! HE'S—
NO, NO. LISTEN. THAT ROCKET SHIP HE CAME IN...YOU KNOW HOW I THOUGHT IT MIGHT BE GERMAN? OR JAPANESE?
I'VE TAKEN A GOOD LONG LOOK AT THE ***PARTS*** THAT WE WERE ABLE TO SALVAGE, MARTHA, AND I CAN GUARANTEE IT DIDN'T JUST COME ACROSS AN ***OCEAN.*** IT CAME FROM—

PLEASE, JONATHAN. ***NOT YET.***
MA AND PA WERE A GOOD DISTANCE AWAY, TALKING QUIETLY. THEY DIDN'T THINK I COULD HEAR THEM.
BUT I COULD.

I HEARD EVERY WORD.
YOU WANT ME TO EAT?
ALL RIGHT...IF THAT'S HOW THE DREAM'S SUPPOSED TO GO.
IS THIS CHICKEN SOUP?
SIP.
NOPE. DEFINITELY NOT. IT'S GOOD, THOUGH.
AN OLD FAMILY RECIPE. UNFORTUNATELY, WE DON'T HAVE CHICKENS WHERE WE'RE FROM.
WAIT—I CAN UNDERSTAND YOU! WHO ARE YOU?
HE ASKED WHO WE ARE, LOVE.
BUT THE REAL QUESTION IS... WHO IS HE?
WH-WHAT'S HAPPENING TO ME?
ISN'T IT OBVIOUS? SLOWLY, IMPERFECTLY, BUT INEVITABLY...
YOU'RE REMEMBERING.

LOOK AT THIS BEAUTIFUL NEW JACKET YOUR FATHER BOUGHT FOR YOU!
IT IS BEAUTIFUL...BUT IT SMELLS LIKE *PLASTIC.*
MY OLD JACKET SMELLED LIKE *YOU.*
LAN-SHIN, WHEN I FIRST CAME TO AMERICA, I FELT *LOST,* EVEN IN CHINATOWN. BUT SLOWLY, I FIGURED THINGS OUT.

THE CORNER BAKERY, FOR INSTANCE, SERVED THE BEST EGG TARTS ON *TUESDAYS* BECAUSE THAT WAS THE ONLY DAY THE OWNER'S GRANDFATHER CAME IN TO BAKE.
AND THE WOODEN BENCH AT THE VERY EDGE OF THE PARK WAS THE BEST PLACE FOR YOUR FATHER AND ME TO WATCH THE *SUNSET.*
AND THE GRUMPY LADY WHO RAN THE TEA SHOP WASN'T REALLY GRUMPY AT ALL. SHE WAS ACTUALLY *SWEET* AND *WARMHEARTED,* ONCE YOU GOT TO KNOW HER.
BEFORE I KNEW IT, I'D FALLEN IN LOVE WITH CHINATOWN.

YOU UNDERSTAND? IF YOU LEARN ENOUGH *SECRETS* ABOUT A PLACE, IT BECOMES *HOME.*
GOOD NIGHT, DARLING.
GOOD NIGHT, MA.

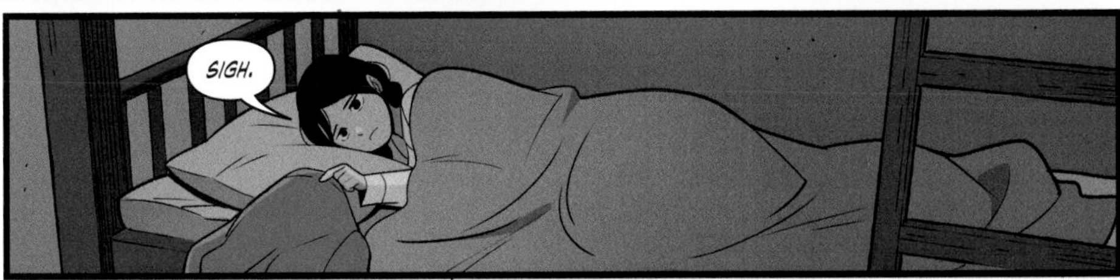
SIGH.

KRKL...
KRKL...
LIGHT...? FROM OUTSIDE...?

KRKL...
KRKL...
KRKL...

TOMMY!
WHO—?!
I-I DON'T KNOW, SIS!

CHILDREN! GET BACK FROM THE WINDOW!
THEY LOOK LIKE GHOSTS!

WE HAVE THEIR ATTENTION, GRAND SCORPION!
MY FELLOW KNIGHTS, I WARNED YOU THAT THESE NON-AMERICANS WOULD NOT BE SATISFIED WITH THEIR OWN FILTHY CORNERS OF OUR CITY!
SOONER OR LATER, THEY WOULD CRAWL OUT TO INFEST OUR LAW ENFORCEMENT, OUR GOVERNMENT, AND OUR VERY NEIGHBORHOODS!
AND THIS PARTICULAR RACE IS A PERPETUAL, UNCHANGING, AND UNCHANGEABLE ALIEN ELEMENT THAT CAN NEVER TRULY BE A PART OF US!

THEIR CULTURE IS DEMORALIZING AND DEGRADING TO OUR PEOPLE! THEY CAN NEVER BECOME ONE HUNDRED PERCENT AMERICANS!
AND SO WE LOYAL KNIGHTS OF THE KLAN OF THE FIERY KROSS MUST PROCLAIM...

ONE RACE! ONE COLOR! ONE RELIGION!

THEY... THEY'VE GOT THE WRONG IDEA ABOUT US, IS ALL! I'LL GO OUT EXPLAIN TO THEM—
ARE YOU OUT OF YOUR MIND?! CALL THE POLICE!
IN ENGLISH, DEAR!
TO HELL WITH YOUR ENGLISH!

TOMMY! NO!
YOU'RE ONLY GOING TO MAKE THINGS WORSE, SON!
THIS IS OUR HOME! THEY'VE GOT NO RIGHT TO BE HERE!

GROWN MEN, PLAYING DRESS-UP AND BURNING CAMPFIRES ON OTHER PEOPLE'S LAWNS? YOU OUGHTA BE ASHAMED!
GET OUTTA HERE BEFORE I CRACK YOUR HEADS OPEN!

WE CAME MERELY TO WARN YOU, ALIEN! YOU FORCE US TO DO MORE!
NEW INITIATE, HAND ME YOUR TORCH!
BUT—

FSSSS...
NEW INITIATE, SHOW THESE NON-AMERICANS WE MEAN BUSINESS!
BUT, GRAND SCORPION, MAYBE THIS ISN'T...
FSSS
THROW IT NOW!
GFN!

BOUNCE!
HE'S GOT ON RED BOOTS.
BOUNCE...
bounce...
bounce...
OH NO...!
RUN FOR COVER!
BOOOOM!

YOU IMBECILE! HOW COULD YOU MISS THE WINDOW?!
I, UH...
IT'S... IT'S THE HOOD! THE HOOD GOT IN THE WAY!

FALL BACK, LOYAL KNIGHTS! WE'VE MADE OUR MESSAGE LOUD AND CLEAR!
THE FIRE'S OUTTA CONTROL!

GRAB BUCKETS! WE GOTTA PUT IT OUT BEFORE IT REACHES THE HOUSE!
TOMMY!

GOOD LORD! A CROSS-BURNING?! HERE IN METROPOLIS?!
YOUNG MAN! YOU GOT A HOSE?!
I SAW ONE AT THE NEIGHBOR'S!

NO, NO! THIS JUST KEEPS GETTING WORSE AND WORSE!

YOU! NOBODY ASKED YOU TO COME HERE! WE DON'T WANT ANY MORE TROUBLE! GET OUT OF HERE!
DAD, THEY'RE TRYING TO HELP!
TROUBLE FOUND YOU, MISTER! WE HAD NOTHING TO DO WITH IT!

NOT HOW I IMAGINED A NIGHT OUT ON THE TOWN WOULD END.
LIKE MY GRANDMA USED TO SAY, NO GOOD DEED GOES UNPUNISHED.
APOLOGIES, BUT CAN YOU FELLAS FIND YOUR OWN WAY HOME? I NEED TO STAY.

YOU HEARD THAT CHINESE GUY, BILL!
THEY DON'T WANT US AROUND, NOT EVEN WHEN THEIR HOUSE IS ON FIRE!
THEY GOT A BURNING CROSS ON THEIR LAWN, DON'T THEY?

FOR TONIGHT, AT LEAST, THEY ARE US.
EVEN IF THEY DON'T WANT TO ADMIT IT.

SIR, I ASKED YOU TO LEAVE US—
OH...!
I'M— I'M—PLEASE FORGIVE ME! I DIDN'T KNOW...

I'M INSPECTOR WILLIAM HENDERSON OF THE METROPOLIS POLICE DEPARTMENT.
HOW ABOUT YOU FOLKS TELL ME WHAT HAPPENED?

THE NEXT MORNING...

LOIS! YOU'RE HERE!

MY TURN TO GET COFFEE.

THANKS. UM, CLARK? NO OFFENSE, BUT DID YOU GET **ANY** SLEEP AT ALL LAST NIGHT? YOUR FACE LOOKS LIKE IT'S BEEN RUN OVER BY A **TRUCK.**

YOU'RE WELCOME FOR THE COFFEE, LOIS.

PERRY SENT ME HERE WITHOUT TELLING ME WHY. ANY IDEAS WHAT—

Metro Café

GREAT SCOTT!

OUR MOST RECOGNIZABLE SYMBOL OF **HATE...**

...RIGHT HERE IN **METROPOLIS.**

MS. LANE! MR. KENT! MR. WHITE GOT MY MESSAGE TO YOU!

NO WAY, JIMMY, YOU KNOW **LOIS LANE** AND **CLARK KENT?!**

SURE. DIDN'T I TELL YOU? I'M A CUB REPORTER AT THE *DAILY PLANET!*

I'D HEARD OF METROPOLIS'S TWO MOST FAMOUS REPORTERS, OF COURSE. ANYONE WHO'S READ THE PAPER HAS. BUT TO ACTUALLY SEE THEM IN PERSON?

WILD. NEVER WOULD'VE HAPPENED IN **CHINATOWN.**

I'M CLARK KENT, REPORTER FOR THE DAILY PLANET.
I-I'M ROBERTA LEE.
HOW'RE YOU HOLDING UP?
ALL RIGHT—COLD—A LITTLE—
...
I MEAN, I'M ALL RIGHT. JUST A LITTLE COLD.
HOW ABOUT YOU BORROW MY JACKET. THAT BETTER?
YEAH.
Metro Café
FOR REASONS I CAN'T QUITE PUT MY FINGER ON, CLARK KENT SEEMS ODDLY FAMILIAR.
Y'KNOW, I ALWAYS KIND OF SUSPECTED THAT I DON'T BELONG.
LAST NIGHT, WE GOT PROOF.
HUSBAND, WE HAVE TO MOVE BACK TO CHINATOWN!
DEAR, WE'RE NOT MOVING AWAY OVER A MISUNDERSTANDING! WE JUST HAVE TO SHOW THEM WE'RE NOT WHAT THEY THINK WE ARE!
YOU HAVE TO DO WHAT'S BEST FOR YOUR FAMILY, OF COURSE, BUT YOU LEAVING IS EXACTLY WHAT THOSE BIGOTS WANT!
IF IT HELPS AT ALL WITH YOUR DECISION, I CAN HAVE A SQUAD CAR IN FRONT OF YOUR HOUSE 24/7.
I CAN'T BELIEVE DAD TOOK THE TIME TO PUT ON HIS LAB COAT.
ROBERTA... WHAT DO YOU WANT?
I DON'T SEE HOW WE CAN STAY. NOT AFTER THIS.
IT MUST'VE BEEN AWFUL LAST NIGHT.

I CAN'T IMAGINE. BUT SHOULD YOUR FAMILY CHOOSE TO STAY, ROBERTA, MR. KENT AND I WILL FIGHT FOR YOU, ONE HUNDRED PERCENT.
THE MEN WHO DID THIS WANT TO KEEP THEIR IDENTITIES SECRET, AND EXPOSING SECRETS IS OUR BUSINESS.
UNLIKE MR. KENT, LOIS LANE IS DECIDEDLY NOT FAMILIAR.
SO SURE OF HERSELF...I'VE NEVER MET ANYONE LIKE HER.
SOMEONE TOLD ME RECENTLY, IF YOU UNCOVER ENOUGH SECRETS ABOUT A PLACE, IT BECOMES HOME.
NOT BAD ADVICE.
COME ON, CLARK. LET'S GO SEE WHAT THE INSPECTOR CAN TELL US.
UNCOVER ENOUGH SECRETS AND YOU MAKE A HOME.
HUH.
THAT'S NOT BAD ADVICE AT ALL, ROBERTA.
MA, DAD... I WANT TO STAY.

"I ALWAYS KIND OF SUSPECTED THAT I DON'T BELONG," ROBERTA SAID.
"LAST NIGHT, WE GOT PROOF."
WITHOUT REALLY MEANING TO, I REMEMBER.
I REMEMBER WHAT I'D VOWED TO FORGET.
SMALLVILLE. 1926.
MY BEST FRIEND PETE ROSS AND I USED TO COLLECT PULP MAGAZINES.
I ESPECIALLY LOVED SCIENCE FICTION STORIES. PETE LIKED ANYTHING CREEPY.
WHOA!
CLARKIE, CHECK THIS ONE OUT!
CREEPIEST ONE YET, RIGHT? HA HA!
THOUGH I DIDN'T REALLY UNDERSTAND WHY, THAT MAGAZINE COVER EMBARRASSED ME.
SUDDENLY, I BEGAN HEARING VOICES, THE SAME VOICES THAT HAD COME FROM THAT PHONOGRAPH-THING PA HAD SHOWN ME A FEW DAYS BEFORE.
YOU ALL RIGHT, CLARKIE? JEEZ, IT'S NOT THAT CREEPY!
I'M ALL RIGHT...
I WAS TOO EMBARRASSED TO ASK IF PETE HEARD THEM, TOO.
I FELT MY FACE GO HOT. NOT MY WHOLE FACE, ACTUALLY.
JUST MY EYES.

KYLE, CHECK THIS OUT!
WHAT KINDA LOSERS READ THIS STUFF?
HEY! YOU GIVE THAT BACK!
Stories of Tomorrow
STOP...
KYLE AND KENNY BRAVERMAN WERE THE NEIGHBORHOOD BULLIES.

OUR DAD SAYS THESE SORTSA MAGAZINES ROT A KID'S BRAIN!
WE'RE GONNA DO YOU A FAVOR, LOSER!
NO!
RIIIIP!
HNN...

KYLE, YOU SEE THAT? THE LOSER TRIED TO PUNCH ME!
WE'LL HAFTA TEACH HIM A LESSON!
NO! LEMME GO!
PLEASE...
RNN...

LEAVE HIM ALONE...
RGH...

CLARKIE? ARE YOU...
FLYING?
I SAID...
RFF...

LEAVE HIM ALONE!
ZZZAAAAPPPPPPPRKTTTT!
AAAH!

HUFF
HUFF
PETE...
WHUH... WHUH...
WHAT—

YOU OKAY?
G-G-GET AWAY FROM ME!

I, TOO, ALWAYS SUSPECTED THAT I DIDN'T **BELONG.**

THAT DAY, I GOT **PROOF.**
ALIEN TALES

I WANTED TO SPEND THE DAY AT HOME, BUT TOMMY INSISTED WE VISIT THE *UNITY HOUSE.*
THE UNITY HOUSE OF METROPOLIS
WE READ ABOUT WHAT HAPPENED IN THE MORNING EDITION!
IT'S JUST TERRIBLE, TOMMY! DID THEY HURT YOU?
NAH. THEY JUST SHOOK US UP A LITTLE.
THE KLAN OF THE FIERY KROSS INVADES METROPOLIS!
ACTUALLY, WHEN WE FIRST SAW THEM THROUGH THE WINDOW, MY MOM THOUGHT THEY WERE GHOSTS!
AND I SAID, "COME ON, MOM! METROPOLIS DOESN'T CELEBRATE HALLOWEEN *THAT* EARLY!"
HEH. HEH.
THEN THEY LIT THAT *FIRE!* BUT BELIEVE ME, *THESE WONTONS* DON'T FRY UP *THAT* EASY!
HA HA HA!
YOU'RE HILARIOUS, TOMMY!
DID HE REALLY JUST CALL US *WONTONS?*
THE CREEPS UNDERNEATH THOSE HOODS COULD HAVE BEEN *ANYONE.* THEY COULD HAVE BEEN FROM THESE KIDS' FAMILIES.
HECK, THEY COULD HAVE BEEN THESE KIDS *THEMSELVES.*
BUT TOMMY'S TOO IMPRESSED BY HIS OWN JOKES TO EVEN THINK ABOUT THAT.

CHUCK RIGGS. WAKE UP.

I'VE JUST BEEN INFORMED BY ONE OF OUR LOYAL KNIGHTS THAT THE LEES HAVE CHOSEN TO IGNORE OUR WARNING.
I CAN'T HELP BUT WONDER IF YOUR INCOMPETENCE LAST NIGHT HAD ANY INFLUENCE ON THEIR DECISION.
I KNOW I DISAPPOINTED YOU, UNCLE MATT... I'M SORRY.

THEN YOU ARE FORGIVEN, YOUNG MAN. IT TAKES TIME AND EFFORT TO BUILD CHARACTER.
EVERY ONE OF US MAKES MISTAKES. WHY, I BET EVEN YOUR HERO HAS MADE HIS SHARE.
SUPERMAN? NAH.

I KNOW YOU WON'T LET ME DOWN AGAIN.
UNCLE MATT? I WAS THINKING, MAYBE IT WAS ENOUGH TO SCARE THEM A LITTLE—

OH, DON'T YOU WORRY ABOUT THE LEES. THE KLAN OF THE FIERY KROSS IS AN OLD AND VENERABLE ORGANIZATION.
CROSS-BURNING ISN'T OUR ONLY RITUAL TO TAKE CARE OF VERMIN.

THOSE UNITY HOUSE KIDS ARE PRETTY GREAT, AREN'T THEY?
I GUESS.

WHAT'S WRONG WITH *YOU?*
I DON'T KNOW...
I MISS CHINATOWN.

A WORD OF ADVICE, SIS? YOU'LL NEVER BE HAPPY IN ***METROPOLIS*** IF YOU KEEP PINING AFTER ***CHINATOWN.***
PSH. AT LEAST ***THERE,*** YOU WEREN'T ***SO FAKE.***

WHAT'S ***THAT*** SUPPOSED TO MEAN?!
"THESE WONTONS DON'T FRY UP ***THAT*** EASY!"
ANYTHING TO FIT IN, RIGHT, TOMMY?!

YOU KNOW WHAT YOUR PROBLEM IS?!
I'M SURE YOU ***CAN'T WAIT*** TO TELL ME!

YOU'RE ALWAYS THINKING ABOUT HOW YOU *DON'T* FIT IN!
MAYBE IF YOU WEREN'T SO *STUCK UP* ABOUT BEING DIFFERENT, YOU'D START MAKING FRIENDS HERE, TOO!

OH, DON'T YOU START *CRYING* ON ME!
YOU'RE THE ONE WHO STARTED IT, CALLING ME *FAKE!*

GO AHEAD AND WALK HOME BY YOURSELF!
SEE IF I CARE!

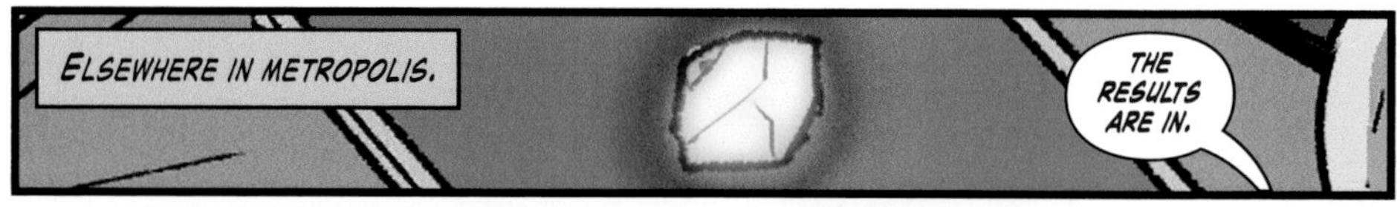
ELSEWHERE IN METROPOLIS.
THE RESULTS ARE IN.

THE GREEN CRYSTAL WE EXTRACTED FROM THE GERMAN'S POWER SOURCE IS, IN FACT, EXTRATERRESTRIAL IN ORIGIN.

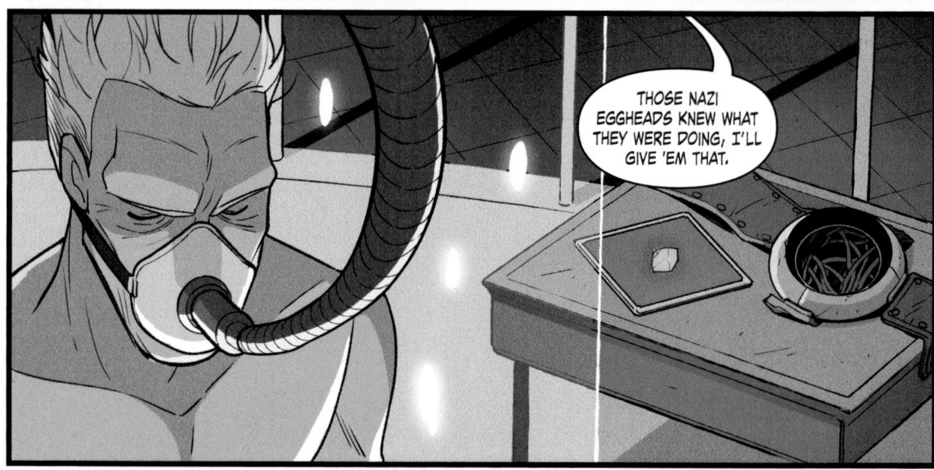
THOSE NAZI EGGHEADS KNEW WHAT THEY WERE DOING, I'LL GIVE 'EM THAT.

WE MAY HAVE BEATEN THEM IN THE WAR, BUT THEY BEAT US TO THE CITY'S—PERHAPS THE WORLD'S—GREATEST SECRET!

CALL ME FAKE, WILL YA...
GRUMBLE GRUMBLE

SQUEEE

YOUNG MAN.
YOU LOOK LIKE YOU'RE A ***LONG WAY*** FROM WHERE YOU BELONG. CAN WE GIVE YOU A RIDE?
THAT'S GENEROUS OF YOU, SIR, BUT NO THANKS.
MY HOUSE IS JUST UP AHEAD.

A *CHING-CHONG* LIVING IN A NEIGHBORHOOD LIKE *THIS?*
YOU DON'T SAY.
!

TOMMY SHOULD'VE BEEN HOME AN HOUR AGO. HE DOESN'T WALK *THAT* SLOW.

MY STOMACH TIGHTENS UP LIKE I'M ABOUT TO GO ON A REALLY, REALLY *BUMPY RIDE.*

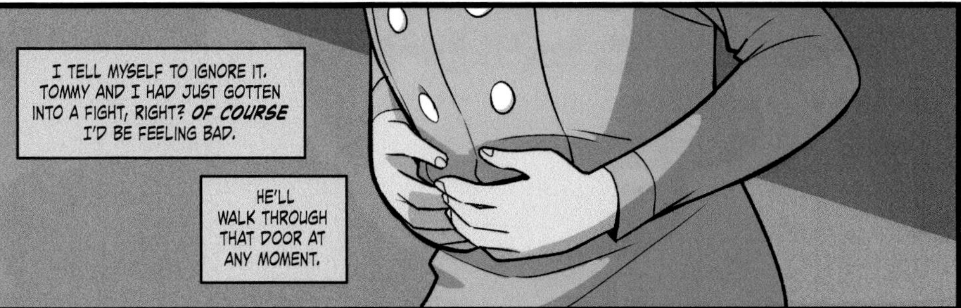
I TELL MYSELF TO IGNORE IT. TOMMY AND I HAD JUST GOTTEN INTO A FIGHT, RIGHT? *OF COURSE* I'D BE FEELING BAD.
HE'LL WALK THROUGH THAT DOOR AT ANY MOMENT.

BUT I DON'T BELIEVE ME.

TOMMY?
TOMMY!
TOMMY LEE!

GASP!

OFFICER! OFFICER!

YOU GOTTA HELP ME!

MY BROTHER, TOMMY LEE—I THINK SOMETHING TERRIBLE HAPPENED TO HIM!

THE DAILY PLANET.

1 · 10 · 20 · 30 · 40 · 50 · 60 · 70 · 77
DING!

JIMMY! ARE YOU HERE?!
CAN I SEE JIMMY OLSEN, PLEASE?!

ROBERTA?!
TOMMY DIDN'T COME HOME, JIMMY! I WENT TO LOOK FOR HIM AND FOUND THIS ON THE SIDE OF THE ROAD!
HE LOVES THIS BASEBALL CAP! HE WOULD NEVER JUST LEAVE IT LIKE THAT!

AW, JEEZ...!

I WANT TO KNOW WHERE CHUCK RIGGS LIVES!
NOW, WAIT A MINUTE...I KNOW HE'S A SOREHEAD AND ALL, BUT YOU DON'T THINK—
TAKE ME TO HIM! PLEASE!

MY SCOOTER'S PARKED IN THE BACK!

GREAT CAESAR'S GHOST—! OLSEN! WHAT'D I TELL YOU ABOUT RUNNING IN MY OFFICE?!
BUMP!
SORRY, CHIEF! WON'T HAPPEN AGAIN!

AND WHAT'D I TELL YOU ABOUT CALLING ME CHIEF?!
THAT WON'T HAPPEN AGAIN EITHER, CHIEF—
I MEAN, MR. WHITE!

KENT! THAT GIRL WITH OLSEN...ISN'T SHE ONE OF THE LEES, FROM THE FRONT PAGE THIS MORNING?
I BELIEVE THAT WAS ROBERTA LEE, DR. LEE'S DAUGHTER.

WELL, WHAT AM I PAYING YOU FOR, KENT?! GO FIGURE OUT WHAT THEIR STORY IS!
RIGHT AWAY, CHIEF!
WHAT'D I JUST SAY ABOUT CALLING ME CHIEF?!

WHERE ARE YOU TAKING ME?!
THIS'LL BE QUITE THE **HONOR** FOR YOU, BOY. YOU'RE ABOUT TO TAKE PART IN AN **OLD KLAN RITUAL.**

FIRST, WE'LL POUR **HOT, STICKY TAR** ON YOU.
SOME FOLKS DIE FROM THE **BURNS,** BUT YOU'RE YOUNG AND STURDY. I EXPECT YOU'LL **SURVIVE.**

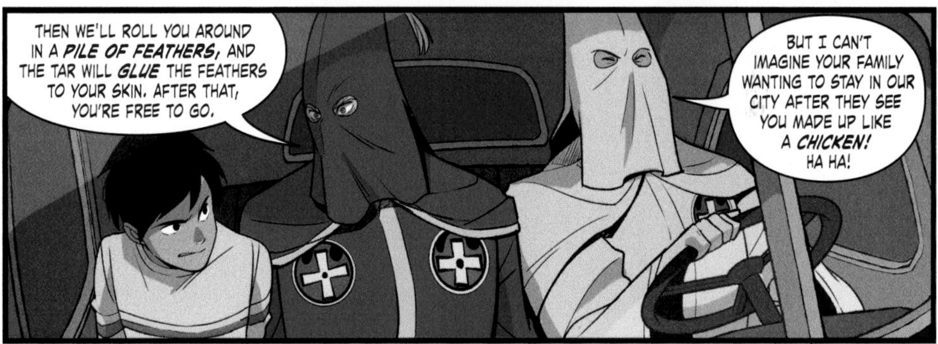
THEN WE'LL ROLL YOU AROUND IN A **PILE OF FEATHERS,** AND THE TAR WILL **GLUE** THE FEATHERS TO YOUR SKIN. AFTER THAT, YOU'RE FREE TO GO.
BUT I CAN'T IMAGINE YOUR FAMILY WANTING TO STAY IN OUR CITY AFTER THEY SEE YOU MADE UP LIKE A **CHICKEN!** HA HA!

BEFORE WE GET STARTED, THOUGH, I WANT YOU TO KNOW THAT WE DON'T **HATE** YOUR KIND.
DON'T YOU BELIEVE THE PAPERS. THERE'S NOT AN **OUNCE OF HATE** IN OUR HEARTS.

IT'S JUST... I'VE SEEN **PHOTOS** OF CHINATOWN. CROWDED, RUN-DOWN, DRUG ADDICTS ON EVERY CORNER... AND MY GOD, **THE FILTH!**
YOU PEOPLE HAVE EVERY RIGHT TO LIVE HOW YOU WANT IN YOUR OWN COUNTRY, BUT I WILL **NOT** PERMIT YOU TO BRING YOUR FILTH INTO **MY COUNTRY,** UNDERSTAND?
IT'S **NOT** LIKE THAT!

WHAM!
GFK!
WHUMP!
OW
SCREEEEECH!
OW
OW
OW
WHY THAT LITTLE—
HE COULDN'T HAVE GOTTEN FAR!
THERE, GRAND SCORPION!

HUFF
HUFF
LEAVE ME ALONE!
DID YOU HURT YOUR ARM, ALIEN? COME OVER HERE AND LET ME TAKE A LOOK.
BLASTED—!
SPLASH!
NO! I—!
GLRGL-
GLRGL-
HA! WITH HIS ARM ALL BUSTED UP, THAT CHING-CHONG'S AS GOOD AS FINISHED!
YES, HE IS. LET'S HEAD BACK.

LOIS LANE SAID EXPOSING SECRETS IS HER BUSINESS.
POUND! POUND! POUND!

IT HAS TO BE MY BUSINESS NOW, TOO.
CHINA GIRL...?
MY NAME IS ROBERTA!

TOMMY WENT MISSING! TELL ME WHAT YOU KNOW!
WHAT?! WHAT MAKES YOU THINK—
I KNOW YOU WERE AT OUR HOUSE LAST NIGHT!

I KNOW YOU WERE THE ONE WHO THREW THE BOMB!
Y-YOU'RE CRAZY!

YOU SHOULD'VE TAKEN OFF YOUR RED BOOTS BEFORE PUTTING ON THAT ROBE, CHUCK.

I'M WARNING YOU!

KRACK!

NO... I DIDN'T MEAN TO ACTUALLY HIT—

SUPERMAN?!

HIYA, SUPERMAN!

HE'S EVEN BIGGER UP CLOSE.

SUPERMAN! I SWEAR I DIDN'T MEAN TO—
ARE YOU ALL RIGHT...?

BETTER THAN YOUR BAT, KID. YOU COULD'VE REALLY HURT SOMEONE!
TELL ME YOUR NAME.
CHUCK RIGGS.
W-WOULD YOU BELIEVE I'M YOUR BIGGEST FAN?
SO THAT'S WHY YOU WEAR THOSE RED BOOTS!

I HOPE YOU DON'T MIND ME EAVESDROPPING, CHUCK.
BUT IT SEEMS TO ME THAT, IF YOU MIGHT BE ABLE TO HELP ANOTHER PERSON, YOU OUGHT TO AT LEAST TRY.
...

I...
I KNOW WHERE THE *KLAN OF THE FIERY KROSS* DOES ITS RITUALS. I CAN SHOW YOU.
MAYBE THEY TOOK TOMMY THERE?

LET'S GO! WE'RE TALKING ABOUT MY BROTHER'S *LIFE* HERE!
I CAN TAKE YOU, BUT I'LL HAVE TO CARRY ONE OF YOU UNDER EACH ARM. IT'LL BE *AWKWARD.*
YOU KNOW THAT LITTLE WOODEN BRIDGE JUST OUTSIDE THE CITY? WE SHOULD HEAD THAT WAY.

JIMMY, CAN YOU GO TELL INSPECTOR HENDERSON WHAT WE'RE UP TO?
YOU BET, SUPERMAN!

YOU TWO READY?
YEAH.
READY.

I'M *ROBERTA LEE,* BY THE WAY. TOMMY'S SISTER.
HANG TIGHT, ROBERTA.

"LET'S GO FIND YOUR BROTHER."

YOU KNOW HOW I TOLD SUPERMAN THAT I WAS READY?
COMPLETE LIE.
I THINK I'M GOING TO BE SICK.

ALIEN TALES

CHAPTER 2

GASP
NHH...
THERE, SUPERMAN! OVER THAT RIVER! THAT'S WHERE THE MEETING WAS!
THE MEETING OF BIGOTS IN BEDSHEETS, CHUCK?
HEY, I'M ALREADY TRYING TO HELP! YOU DON'T HAVE TO BE SO DISRESPECTFUL OF—
KIDS, LET'S STAY FOCUSED ON FINDING TOMMY!
HANG TIGHT!
UH, SUPERMAN? PLEASE DON'T TELL ME YOU'RE GONNA—

HA HA!
LEAP!

—JUMP OVER THAT RIVER!

NOBODY'S HERE. I THOUGHT FOR ***SURE...***

LOOK! THESE TIRE TRACKS ARE ***FRESH!***

WHOEVER MADE THEM MIGHT STILL BE AROUND!

I LISTEN FOR A CAR ENGINE, FOOTSTEPS, VOICES...

NOTHING.

DON'T JUST LISTEN.

LOOK.
YOU TWO!
UH...WHAT'D YOU JUST SAY, SUPERMAN?

ROBERTA, CHUCK, DO EITHER OF YOU HAPPEN TO SEE...
NO, NO.
TOMMY?! YOU SEE TOMMY SOMEWHERE?
WHERE?!
HOW CAN THIS BE? I'M *AWAKE* NOW!

FOR JUST A MOMENT, THE ROCKS, THE BUSHES, EVEN THE GROUND I'M STANDING ON—
—ALL LOOK AS IF THEY'RE MADE OF GLASS.
HE'S IN THE RIVER!

SEEING THROUGH ROCKS—

—I SHOULDN'T BE ABLE TO DO THAT.
TOMMY!
OH, THANK GOD!

TOMMY...?
SAY SOMETHING!

COUGH! COUGH!
HOW COME YOUR BREATH...
SMELLS LIKE BARF...?

DUMMY. I'M SO HAPPY YOU'RE ALIVE I'M GONNA LET THAT ONE GO.
OW! MY ARM!
CAREFUL, ROBERTA! IT MIGHT BE BROKEN!

YOU CAN KNOW FOR SURE. TAKE A LOOK AT HIS BONE.
LOOK THROUGH.
WHOA... SUPERMAN'S HERE?!
THEY'RE STILL HERE.
MINDING YOURSELF TOO MUCH IS A GOOD WAY TO LOSE YOUR MIND, CLARK.

STAY FOCUSED ON TOMMY.
TOMMY, WHEN YOU TRY TO MOVE IT, DOES IT FEEL LIKE THE WORST PAIN EVER?
HNN... PRETTY MUCH...
I BET IT'S BROKEN. WE GOTTA GET THAT ARM IN A SLING. WE CAN USE MY SHIRT—

NO, LET'S USE MY CAPE.

SUPERMAN! LOOK WHO I BROUGHT WITH ME!
GOOD MAN, JIMMY!

INSPECTOR HENDERSON, I HAVE TO GET TOMMY TO THE HOSPITAL AS QUICK AS I CAN! CAN YOU TAKE CARE OF ROBERTA AND CHUCK?
YOU GOT IT, BIG GUY. NO—

—PROBLEM.
FWOOOSH!

YOU GOTTA DO ***WHAT'S RIGHT,*** CHUCK! TELL US EVERYTHING YOU KNOW ABOUT WHAT HAPPENED TONIGHT!

I TOLD YOU ALREADY, I DON'T KNOW ***NOTHIN',*** JIMMY!

SORRY YOU WON'T BE ABLE TO WRITE A FANCY STORY ABOUT IT FOR THE *PLANET!*

AND, YOUNG MAN... CHUCK. FROM WHAT I SAW, SUPERMAN COULDN'T HAVE SAVED YOUR FRIEND WITHOUT YOU. IS THAT RIGHT?
TOMMY ISN'T HIS FRIEND!
BUT IT'S TRUE. IF CHUCK HADN'T TAKEN US TO THAT SPOT, TOMMY MIGHT NOT HAVE MADE IT.

SEEMS TO ME YOU'VE ALREADY DONE WHAT'S RIGHT.
I'LL TELL YOU WHAT. AFTER I DROP ROBERTA OFF AT THE HOSPITAL, I'LL TAKE YOU BACK TO YOUR HOME. YOU GET A GOOD NIGHT'S REST.
I'LL COME BY IN THE MORNING AND WE CAN HAVE A CHAT.

OKAY BY YOU?
YEAH.
I MEAN, YES.
YES, SIR.

METROPOLIS HOSPITAL.

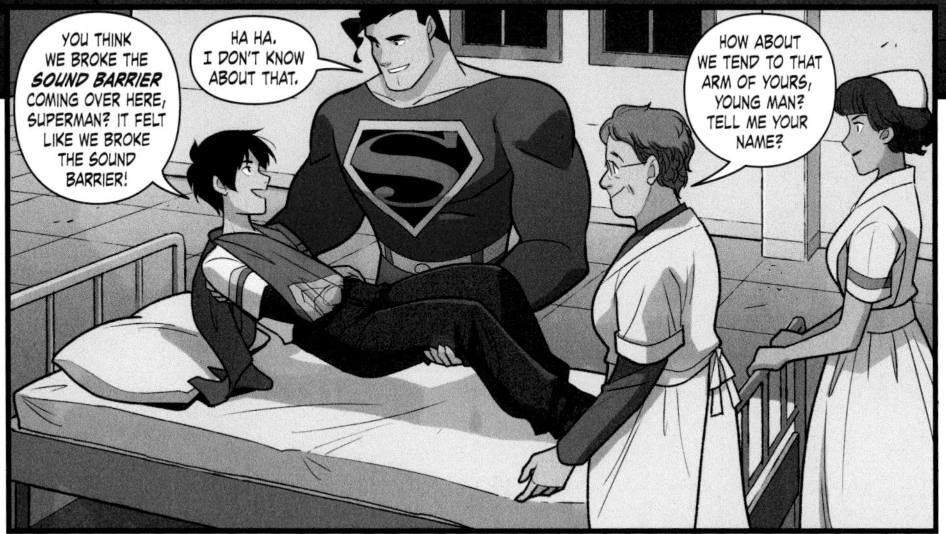
YOU THINK WE BROKE THE SOUND BARRIER COMING OVER HERE, SUPERMAN? IT FELT LIKE WE BROKE THE SOUND BARRIER!
HA HA. I DON'T KNOW ABOUT THAT.
HOW ABOUT WE TEND TO THAT ARM OF YOURS, YOUNG MAN? TELL ME YOUR NAME?

MY NAME'S TOMMY LEE, DOCTOR!
AND I JUST BROKE THE SOUND BARRIER!
THAT'S VERY NICE. NOW, HOW DO WE GET AHOLD OF YOUR PARENTS?

THAT GREEN CRYSTAL SMELL AGAIN.
SNIFF
SNIFF

SIGH.
THEY'VE CHANGED OUTFITS.

SPECTACULAR JOB SAVING THAT BOY!
WE'RE SO *PROUD!*
TELL ME THE TRUTH. ARE YOU SOME SORT OF TRICK BY LUTHOR? OR DER TEUFEL?

BEFORE WE SENT YOU HERE, WE THEORIZED THAT THIS PLANET'S YELLOW SUN WOULD GIVE YOU POWERS BEYOND IMAGINING.
IT SEEMS WE WERE CORRECT.
NO. WHAT YOU'RE SAYING CAN'T BE TRUE!

I—I DON'T LOOK A THING LIKE YOU!
THOUGH YOU WERE IGNORANT OF THEIR SOURCE, YOU'VE ALWAYS KNOWN THAT YOU HAVE POWERS.
YOU ARE OBVIOUSLY STRONGER AND FASTER THAN THEY.

BUT THEN, WHY ARE YOU WILLING TO USE SOME OF YOUR POWERS, BUT NOT OTHERS?
AND JUST LIKE THAT—

MORE MEMORIES COME RUSHING BACK.
SMALLVILLE. 1926.
THAT BOY IS DEMON POSSESSED, I TELL YOU!
HOW ELSE DO YOU EXPLAIN WHAT MY BOYS SAW?!

H-HE FLOATED UP IN THE—
THE BIBLE CALLS IT *LEVITATION.*
HE LEVITATIONED UP IN THE AIR!
AND THE *FIRES OF HELL* SHOT OUT FROM HIS EYES!
PLEASE, MRS. BRAVERMAN, CALM DOWN. I'M SURE WE CAN—

HOW AM I SUPPOSED TO *CALM DOWN* WHEN THERE'S A VERITABLE *DEMON* HERE IN OUR MIDST?!
IT AND ITS HOST MUST BE *EXORCISED* FROM SMALLVILLE!
EVENING, FOLKS.

ABOUT TIME YOU SHOWED UP, SHERIFF!
THE KENT BOY IS POSSESSED BY A *DEMON!* EARLIER TODAY, KENNY AND KYLE SAW HIM PERFORM ALL MANNER OF *SUPERNATURAL DEVILRY!*

SHOULDN'T YOU HAVE CALLED ON PASTOR LEONE INSTEAD?
THAT LOUT IS ALWAYS TRYING TO AVOID ME!
YOU DON'T SAY.

I CAN TAKE IT FROM HERE, MRS. BRAVERMAN. HOW ABOUT YOU ALL HEAD HOME?
GOOD THINKING, SHERIFF!
NEVER KNOW WHEN A POSSESSED BOY MIGHT GET A HANKERING FOR *HUMAN FLESH!*

CLARK KENT.
STEP FORWARD, PLEASE.

SNIFF SNIFF
HM. NOT A HINT OF BRIMSTONE.
HOW ABOUT YOU PERFORM A BIT OF THAT SUPERNATURAL DEVILRY FOR ME, SON?
I'M SORRY, SIR, BUT I—

NOW WAIT ONE MINUTE! ARE YOU TELLING ME THAT YOU ARE ENTIRELY INCAPABLE OF SUPERNATURAL DEVILRY?!
WELL, THEN, I HEREBY DECLARE THAT THIS BOY IS NOT POSSESSED BY A DEMON!

THANK YOU, SHERIFF.
I'VE KNOWN CLARK PRETTY MUCH ALL HIS LIFE, MARTHA. HE'S ALWAYS LOOKING TO HELP, NEVER ANY TROUBLE.
IF THAT BOY'S GOT A DEMON IN HIM, IT'S JUST ABOUT THE LOUSIEST DEMON IN ALL CREATION.

WE APPRECIATE IT, TRULY.
HEY, THIS IS SMALLVILLE. WE LOOK AFTER OUR OWN.
THAT INCLUDES YOU FOLKS, OF COURSE. AND, FOR BETTER OR WORSE, THAT INCLUDES THE BRAVERMANS, TOO.
I'LL GO SEE IF I CAN TALK SOME SENSE INTO 'EM.

LATER THAT NIGHT...
MA... CAN I ASK YOU SOMETHING?
WHAT IF THE BRAVERMANS ARE RIGHT? I MEAN, I ACTUALLY DID LEVITATE, AND...AND...
CLARK. PLEASE.
"WOE UNTO THEM THAT CALL EVIL GOOD, AND GOOD EVIL."
YOU OUGHT TO WORRY LESS ABOUT YOU AND MORE ABOUT THOSE POOR BRAVERMAN BOYS. SEEMS TO ME THEY'VE GOT A LIFETIME OF WOE AHEAD OF THEM.

BUT HOW ELSE DO YOU EXPLAIN WHAT HAPPENED? WHAT I DID? MA...
WHAT AM I?

YOU ARE OUR SON, CLARK KENT. THAT'S ALL YOU NEED TO KNOW.
FOR NOW, AT LEAST.
NOW GET SOME SLEEP.

BUT THAT WASN'T ALL I NEEDED TO KNOW.

I SNUCK INTO PA'S WORK SHED FOR A CLOSER LOOK AT THE ONLY CLUE I HAD.

IF I COULD HEAR THOSE WEIRD VOICES AGAIN, I THOUGHT, I MIGHT BE ABLE TO MAKE SENSE OF THEM.
I MIGHT BE ABLE TO MAKE SENSE OF ME.

BUT I COULDN'T GET THE THING TO TURN ON.
TAP
TAP
TAP

I DECIDED TO BRING IT TO PA. SURE, IT WAS LATE, BUT HE'D NEVER BEEN ONE TO TURN AWAY MY CURIOSITY.

I COULD HEAR THEM THROUGH THE WINDOW.
MUCH AS I HATE TO ADMIT IT, YOU WERE RIGHT, JONATHAN. IT'S TIME TO TELL HIM WHAT WE KNOW ABOUT... YOU KNOW. THE TRUTH.
NO, MARTHA. I WAS WRONG. WE'VE ALREADY TOLD HIM TOO MUCH.

I NEVER SHOULD'VE SHOWN HIM THAT BOX WITH THE VOICES! WHAT IF THAT'S WHAT TRIGGERED ALL THIS STRANGE BEHAVIOR?
BUT THOSE AWFUL PEOPLE PUT IT IN HIS HEAD THAT HE MIGHT BE DEMON POSSESSED!
WE HAVE TO SHOW HIM THAT HE'S NOT! THAT HE'S—

WHAT, MARTHA? SAY IT.
AN ALIEN?
I WOULD NEVER USE THAT WORD FOR OUR CLARK!

THERE ARE FOLKS OUT THERE MUCH MORE DANGEROUS THAN THE BRAVERMANS. IF THEY WERE TO DISCOVER THAT OUR SON IS AN—
THAT HE'S EXTRAORDINARY, THEY MIGHT TAKE HIM AWAY. OR WORSE.
I REFUSE TO LET THAT HAPPEN.
FROM NOW ON, CLARK MUST BE ORDINARY. NO MORE INCIDENTS. NO MORE UNWANTED ATTENTION.

WE'LL RAISE HIM TO BE THE MOST PERFECTLY ORDINARY BOY IN ALL OF SMALLVILLE.
AGREED?
... AGREED.

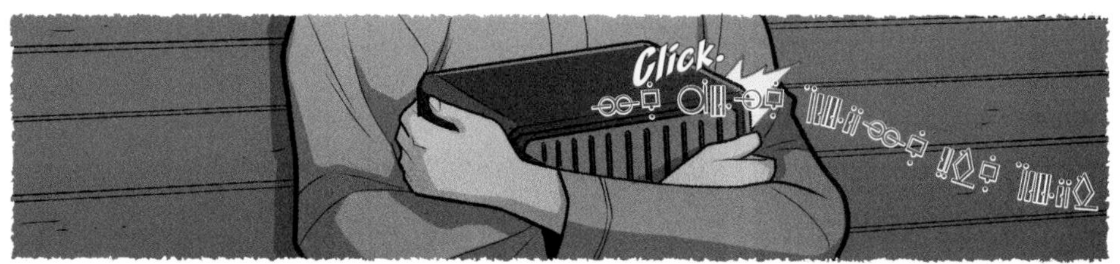
Click.

GASP!
NO NO NO!
SHUT UP
SHUT UP
SHUT UP!

CLARK...?
IS THAT YOU?
VOOOSH!

VOOOSH!
NO NO NO!

SHUT UP!
SHUT UP!

SHUT UP!
TOSS

KRKL
SPLASH

HUFF
HUFF

PLEASE...
HUFF
LET ME BE ORDINARY.
PERFECTLY ORDINARY.

PERFECT.

THE NEXT MORNING, WE SAT DOWN FOR BREAKFAST, JUST LIKE ALWAYS.
WE SMILED AND ATE AND TALKED ABOUT THE DAY AHEAD.
NO ONE BROUGHT UP THE NIGHT BEFORE.

WHY, SON? WHY SOME POWERS, BUT NOT OTHERS?
IT'S AS IF YOU ONLY WANT TO BE HALF OF WHO YOU ACTUALLY ARE.

HOW ABOUT YOU SIGN IT, "TO MY DEAREST TOMMY, THE SMARTEST PERSON IN THE LEE FAMILY!"
NOPE.
TOMMY! ROBERTA, YOU'RE HERE, TOO! OH, THANK GOODNESS!
AFTER THE LAST NIGHT, YOUR FATHER AND I FEARED THE WORST!

WHERE WERE YOU CHILDREN?! HOW COULD THIS HAVE HAPPENED?!
DOES IT HURT?
EH. A LITTLE, BUT TOTALLY WORTH IT! YOU SEE, SUPERMAN—

SUPERMAN DID THIS?!
I KNEW HIS "GOOD CITIZEN" ACT WOULDN'T LAST! A BEING THAT POWERFUL COULD NEVER—

DAD, YOU'VE GOT IT ALL WRONG! SUPERMAN DIDN'T HURT TOMMY—HE SAVED HIS LIFE!
WITH ROBERTA'S HELP.

THANKS, SIS.
...
YOU WOULD'VE DONE THE SAME FOR ME.
YEAH. I WOULD'VE.

BUT THEN WHO HURT YOU, SON?! WAS IT THOSE TERRIBLE MEN IN HOODS?
UH, WELL...
NAH! I WAS, UH, GOOFING AROUND BY THE RIVER AND SORT OF FELL IN! LIKE A DUMMY! HA HA!
?!
WHY WOULD HE LIE ABOUT THE KLAN OF THE FIERY KROSS?!

UM...YUP! HE JUST FELL IN LIKE A DUMMY! HA HA! LIKE THE BIGGEST DUMMY EVER!
WELL, I WOULDN'T SAY THE BIGGEST EVER! HA HA! ACTUALLY, GIVEN THE LIGHTING, IT WAS ALL PRETTY UNDERSTANDABLE!
STILL, GOOD THING SUPERMAN HAPPENED BY!

BUT THE RIVER IS MILES AWAY FROM OUR HOME! WHY WOULD YOU BE ANYWHERE NEAR—
H-HEY, YOU KNOW WHAT? WE SHOULD PROBABLY GIVE SUPERMAN HIS CAPE BACK!
HE'S STILL HERE?!

SURE. I CAN SEE HIM FROM THE WINDOW.

BUT HOW IS THIS HAPPENING? ARE YOU GHOSTS? SOME SORT OF PROJECTION?
EXCUSE ME, SUPERMAN?
ROBERTA!
I'M NOT INTERRUPTING ANYTHING, AM I?
IS SUPERMAN TALKING TO HIMSELF?
NO, NO! JUST...ENJOYING THE NIGHT AIR! HOW'S TOMMY?
HE'S PRETTY EXCITED ABOUT BRAGGING TO THE UNITY HOUSE THAT HE MET YOU.
IN OTHER WORDS, HE'S FINE.
MR. SUPERMAN?

MRS. AND DR. LEE, I PRESUME?
THANK YOU, MR. SUPERMAN! OUR SON IS ALIVE AND SAFE! THANK YOU! THANK YOU!
YOUR CHILDREN ARE SO COURAGEOUS! YOU MUST BE PROUD!
MY WIFE AND I TRULY ARE GRATEFUL TO YOU, SUPERMAN.
HERE'S YOUR CAPE BACK.
...
CAN I LET YOU IN ON A SECRET, ROBERTA? CRIME-FIGHTING CAN BE PRETTY ROUGH ON CAPES, SO MY MOTHER MADE ME A WHOLE CLOSETFUL OF THESE.
I'D LIKE YOU TO KEEP THIS ONE.
WHAT?! REALLY?!
IS TOMMY RIGHT?
IS EVERYTHING WE'VE GONE THROUGH IN METROPOLIS WORTH IT FOR THIS ONE MOMENT?
AFTER ALL, YOU'RE THE REAL HERO TONIGHT!
I THINK I'M GONNA HAVE TO SAY YES.

THE NEXT MORNING. THE DAILY PLANET.
PERRY?
YOU WANTED TO SEE ME?
IT'S YOUR STORY ABOUT WHAT HAPPENED LAST NIGHT, KENT.
YOU NEED A REWRITE? I'D BE HAPPY TO—
THAT'S NOT WHAT I'M GETTING AT. IT'S TREMENDOUS.
SO GOOD, IN FACT, I THOUGHT LOIS HAD WRITTEN IT.
UM... THANKS?
IT'S JUST... THE KLAN OF THE FIERY KROSS KIDNAPPED A KID?
HERE IN METROPOLIS?!
GREAT CAESAR'S GHOST, IS THIS REALLY MY CITY?!
BUT THEY DIDN'T GET AWAY WITH IT, RIGHT? SUPERMAN—
THAT'S JUST IT. SUPERMAN DID SOMETHING.
AND SO SHOULD WE.

MY, MY.

Daily Planet

DAILY PLANET

$1000 REWARD FOR KLAN OF THE FIERY KROSS

After second Klan attack, Daily Planet offers reward for information leading to arrest of Klan leader!

WITH A THOUSAND DOLLARS WE COULD GET OUT OF YOUR UNCLE'S HAIR AND RENT OUR OWN PLACE, CHUCK!

TELL ME, WHAT DO YOU KNOW ABOUT ***THE KLAN OF THE FIERY KROSS?***

M-M-MOM?! W-W-WHY WOULD YOU—?!

UNCLE MATT! YOU SEE THIS?!
WHAT?

OH, HELL.
WHAT'S THIS YOU'RE WORKING ON?

UNCLE MATT... WHAT HAPPENED TO TOMMY LEE LAST NIGHT... THAT WASN'T YOU, RIGHT?
THAT MUST'VE BEEN SOME OF THE OTHER KNIGHTS.
RIGHT?
NOT NOW, CHUCK. WE HAVE VISITORS.

HOW'D THE COPS KNOW TO COME HERE?!

WELL...
MAYBE...
UM...

A WORD OF ADVICE, CHUCK: STAY AWAY FROM THE UNITY HOUSE.

AFTER ALL...

WE'RE AT WAR.

AND I DON'T WANT MY NEPHEW GETTING CAUGHT IN THE CROSSFIRE.

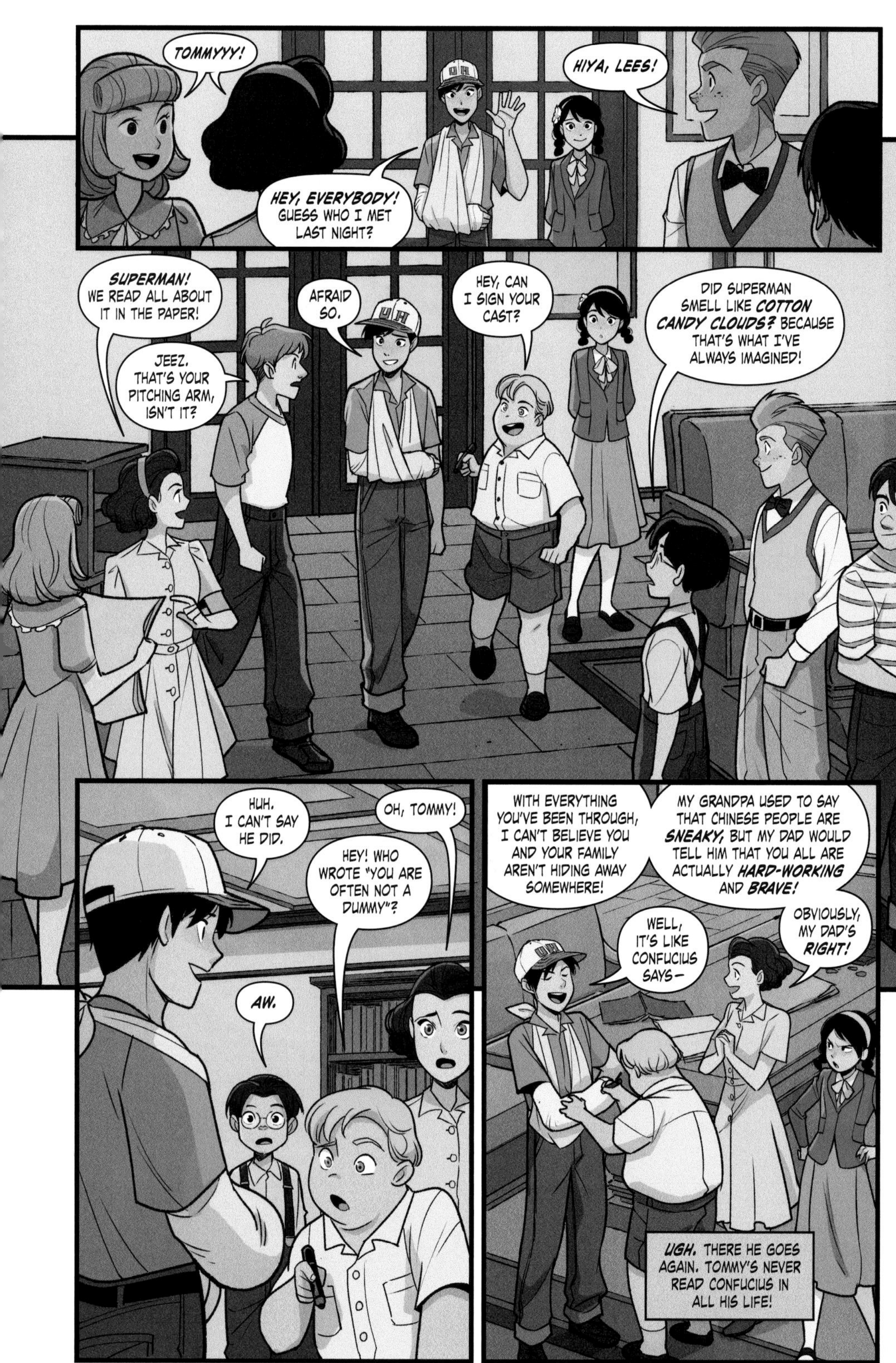

TOMMYYY!
HEY, EVERYBODY! GUESS WHO I MET LAST NIGHT?
HIYA, LEES!
SUPERMAN! WE READ ALL ABOUT IT IN THE PAPER!
JEEZ. THAT'S YOUR PITCHING ARM, ISN'T IT?
AFRAID SO.
HEY, CAN I SIGN YOUR CAST?
DID SUPERMAN SMELL LIKE COTTON CANDY CLOUDS? BECAUSE THAT'S WHAT I'VE ALWAYS IMAGINED!
HUH. I CAN'T SAY HE DID.
OH, TOMMY!
HEY! WHO WROTE "YOU ARE OFTEN NOT A DUMMY"?
AW.
WITH EVERYTHING YOU'VE BEEN THROUGH, I CAN'T BELIEVE YOU AND YOUR FAMILY AREN'T HIDING AWAY SOMEWHERE!
MY GRANDPA USED TO SAY THAT CHINESE PEOPLE ARE SNEAKY, BUT MY DAD WOULD TELL HIM THAT YOU ALL ARE ACTUALLY HARD-WORKING AND BRAVE!
WELL, IT'S LIKE CONFUCIUS SAYS—
OBVIOUSLY, MY DAD'S RIGHT!
UGH. THERE HE GOES AGAIN. TOMMY'S NEVER READ CONFUCIUS IN ALL HIS LIFE!

WE'RE NOT ALL *BRAVE*, Y'KNOW. OR *SNEAKY*.
WE'RE NOT ALL *ANYTHING!*

SUPERMAN GAVE ME HIS CAPE. OUR MOM MADE IT INTO THIS JACKET.
YOUR MOM SEWED THAT?!
IT'S BEAUTIFUL!
NO WAY!
MY SOCKS ARE OFFICIALLY KNOCKED OFF!
MIND IF I CHECK IF IT SMELLS LIKE COTTON CANDY CLOUDS?
DON'T BE WEIRD!
I THINK I'VE FIGURED OUT WHY TOMMY DIDN'T TELL OUR PARENTS ABOUT THE KLAN. DESPITE EVERYTHING THAT'S HAPPENED, HE DOESN'T WANT TO LEAVE.
AND I GET IT. HERE IN METROPOLIS, OUR LIVES SOMEHOW FEEL BIGGER.
IT LOOKS GREAT ON YOU, ROBERTA. BETTER THAN ON SUPERMAN, EVEN.
BUT DON'T TELL HIM I SAID THAT.
THANKS, JIMMY.
AND I WON'T.
FOR THE FIRST TIME SINCE WE MOVED, I DON'T FEEL LIKE SUCH A WEIRDO.

EVERYBODY LISTEN TO ME—!
HEY! IT'S CHUCK!
CHUCK RIGGS?! YOU GOT A LOT OF NERVE SHOWING UP HERE!
HUFF HUFF
PLEASE—!
FOLKS, LET'S HEAR HIM OUT.
WAIT. YOU'RE FRIENDS WITH THAT SOREHEAD AGAIN?!
WELL... "FRIENDS" IS KIND OF PUSHING IT.
SURE, WE'RE FRIENDS! CHUCK HELPED SUPERMAN SAVE ME LAST NIGHT, TOO!
IS THAT TRUE?
YEAH— I GUESS— LISTEN!
WE GOTTA GET OUTTA HERE! THIS BUILDING, I MEAN!
WHY?
WELL...UM...IT— IT'S SUCH A BEAUTIFUL DAY... RIGHT? WHY STAY INSIDE?
HEY, I GOT IT! HOW ABOUT WE GO PRACTICE?! TOMMY CAN SHOW US THAT SWEET FASTBALL!
TOMMY'S ARM IS BROKEN, CHUCK.
OH. RIGHT.
GASP! YOU HEAR THAT?!
TICK TICK TICK
THAT TICKING?!
WE GOTTA—!

YOU MEAN THE TICKING OF THAT CLOCK?
OH, YEAH. OF COURSE. THE CLOCK. HEH HEH.
TICK TICK TICK
WHAT'S GOTTEN INTO YOU, CHUCK?

HOW ABOUT THIS? MAYBE WE SHOULD, I DON'T KNOW, HEAD OVER TO THE THEATER FOR A MOVIE OR SOMETHING?
HEY, THAT'S A GREAT IDEA!

I'VE BEEN WANTING TO SEE THAT NEW CAPTAIN DESMO FLICK.
SOMETHING'S OFF ABOUT CHUCK. I NEED TO FIGURE OUT WHAT.

I HEARD THE SPECIAL EFFECTS ARE A BLAST!

METROPOLIS HEALTH DEPARTMENT.
MS. LANE! WHAT ARE YOU DOING HERE?
HELLO, DR. LEE!

I'M WORKING ON AN ARTICLE ABOUT ALL THE GOOD WORK YOU'RE DOING HERE AT THE METROPOLIS HEALTH DEPARTMENT.
I'M NOT SURE I CAN STILL CONSIDER OUR WORK HERE "GOOD."

HOW DO YOU MEAN, DR. LEE?
IT'S...IT'S NOTHING.
YOU'LL PROBABLY WANT TO SPEAK WITH DR. WILSON, OUR DEPARTMENT HEAD. HIS OFFICE IS AT THE END OF THAT CORRIDOR.

END OF THE CORRIDOR. GOT IT. THANK YOU!

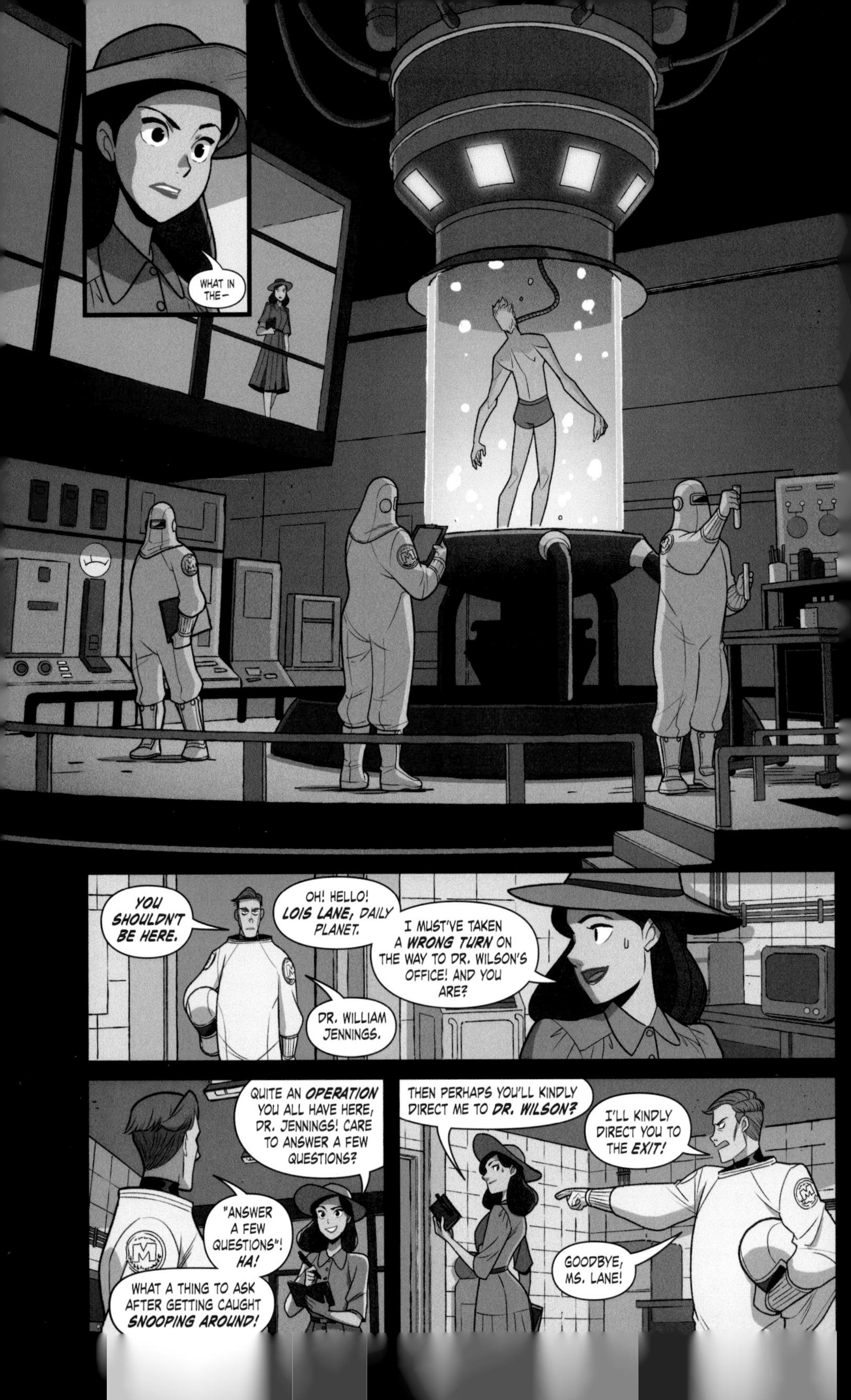
WHAT IN THE—
YOU SHOULDN'T BE HERE.
OH! HELLO! LOIS LANE, DAILY PLANET.
I MUST'VE TAKEN A WRONG TURN ON THE WAY TO DR. WILSON'S OFFICE! AND YOU ARE?
DR. WILLIAM JENNINGS.
QUITE AN OPERATION YOU ALL HAVE HERE, DR. JENNINGS! CARE TO ANSWER A FEW QUESTIONS?
"ANSWER A FEW QUESTIONS"! HA!
WHAT A THING TO ASK AFTER GETTING CAUGHT SNOOPING AROUND!
THEN PERHAPS YOU'LL KINDLY DIRECT ME TO DR. WILSON?
I'LL KINDLY DIRECT YOU TO THE EXIT!
GOODBYE, MS. LANE!

ROBERTA, YOU GOTTA TELL ME! WHAT'S SUPERMAN *REALLY* LIKE?

DID YOU GET A WHIFF OF COTTON CANDY CLOUDS AT ALL?

YOU GOTTA STOP WITH THAT.

HE'S WARM AND KIND, BUT *STRONG* AS ALL GET-OUT! YOU KNOW THE METROPOLIS RIVER? HE LEAPT ACROSS IT IN A *SINGLE BOUND!*

AND YOU ACTUALLY HELPED HIM SAVE YOUR BROTHER?

LIKE I WAS SAYING, YOU CHINESE ARE *SO BRAVE!*

NO, NOT REALLY. TO BE HONEST... I WAS COMPLETELY SCARED THE WHOLE TIME! RIGHT BEFORE WE FOUND TOMMY, I THREW UP INTO A BUSH! RIGHT IN FRONT OF SUPERMAN!
WHICH WAS BETTER THAN THE TIME BEFORE, I GUESS, WHEN I THREW UP ALL OVER MY JACKET AND HANDS!
WHAT I'M SAYING IS, I THROW UP A LOT.
LIKE, A LOT A LOT. IN A NOT-SO-BRAVE WAY.
Y'KNOW. GURGLY STOMACH.

...
...

SOOO...I'M GONNA GO FIND OUT WHAT MOVIE WE'RE WATCHING.
OH.
OKAY.

EXCEPT IT SAYS RIGHT HERE WHAT MOVIE WE'RE GOING TO WATCH.

CAPTAIN DESMO VS. GENGHIS AHKIM
THE INTERGALACTIC CONQUEROR

THEY ARE!
HARRIET! VIVIAN!
MY OLD FRIENDS FROM CHINATOWN!
I'M SO HAPPY TO SEE YOU!
ROBERTA!
IT'S YOU.
COME ON, HARRIET. WE DON'T WANT TO MISS THE OPENING CREDITS.
WHAT'S WRONG WITH HER?
IT ALWAYS SEEMED LIKE SHE DIDN'T LIKE ME.
YOU KNOW HOW VIV IS.
WELL... SHE THOUGHT YOU WERE KIND OF STANDOFFISH. EVERY TIME WE ASKED YOU TO COME TO THE MOVIES WITH US, YOU'D TURN US DOWN.
ONLY BECAUSE THE BUS RIDE WOULD MAKE ME FEEL SICK!
...

YOU SURE IT WASN'T BECAUSE YOU THOUGHT YOU WERE BETTER THAN THE REST OF US?
WHAT?!
YOUR FATHER THE DOCTOR CERTAINLY ACTED THAT WAY.
THAT ISN'T HOW—
THAT'S WHY YOUR FAMILY LEFT CHINATOWN, ISN'T IT?

NO! IT'S—
LOOK, IT'S BEEN SO LONG.
MAYBE WE CAN SIT TOGETHER IN THE THEATER? I REALLY MISS—
YOU'RE HERE WITH YOUR NEW FRIENDS, RIGHT? I'M SURE YOU'D HAVE MORE FUN SITTING WITH THEM.

NICE BUMPING INTO YOU, ROBERTA.
YEAH...
YOU, TOO.

METRO CAFÉ.

THE NAME "METROPOLIS HEALTH DEPARTMENT" MAKES IT SOUND LIKE IT'S A GOVERNMENT OPERATION, RIGHT? BUT IT'S NOT.

AT ALL.

I GOT AHOLD OF THEIR FINANCIAL RECORDS, CLARK. NONE OF THEIR FUNDING COMES FROM THE CITY, NOT ONE DIME!

AND YOU WOULDN'T BELIEVE WHAT I SAW THERE TODAY! LIKE SOME KIND OF MAD SCIENTIST'S LAB!

I SEE HOW ALL THIS MIGHT LEAD TO SOMETHING BIG, LOIS, BUT I'M STILL SURPRISED YOU'RE NOT PUTTING EVERYTHING YOU'VE GOT INTO THE KLAN STORY.

THAT'S THE THING, CLARK. I'VE GOT A HUNCH THAT—
OH NO.

WHAT ARE YOU STARING AT?
THEY'RE APPEARING IN BROAD DAYLIGHT NOW.

MEN CAN ALWAYS FIND NEW WAYS TO DISAPPOINT YOU, CAN'T THEY?
WHAT...?

I GET IT. SHE'S PRETTY. WHY PAY ATTENTION TO A CONVERSATION WITH A *COLLEAGUE* WHEN THERE'S A PRETTY WOMAN ACROSS THE SHOP?
LOIS, I DIDN'T EVEN NOTICE HER!

SURE YOU DIDN'T. GO TALK TO HER, CHAMP.
SOME OF US HAVE WORK TO DO. I'LL SEE YOU BACK AT THE OFFICE.
I PROMISE YOU I WASN'T—

WHO WANTS TO TALK TO A PRETTY WOMAN ACROSS THE SHOP WHEN THE ***PRETTIEST, SMARTEST, MOST FEARLESS WOMAN*** I'VE EVER MET IS RIGHT ACROSS THE TABLE?

HEY! WATCH IT, FELLA!

COME ON.

IF YOU'RE GOING TO SHOW YOURSELVES, SHOW YOURSELVES **NOW.**

THE CITY'S SKYLINE IS SPECTACULAR.
PRIMITIVE, BUT SPECTACULAR.
IS THAT WHY YOU BROUGHT US UP HERE, SON? TO SHOW US THE VIEW?
WE'RE UP HERE BECAUSE I CAN'T BE SEEN TALKING TO MYSELF.
WHAT IS IT THAT YOU WANT?

"WHY ONLY BE HALF OF WHO YOU *ACTUALLY ARE?*"

HEY, DEMON-BOY!

HOW ABOUT YOU LEVA—LEVI—LEVO—

FLOAT FOR US AGAIN, DEMON-BOY?!

YEAH! SHOOT US WITH THEM ***HELLFIRE EYES!***

KYLE, KENNY, ***GO AWAY!***

NOT UNTIL YOU SHOW ALL THESE FINE CHURCH-GOIN' FOLKS YOUR ***TRUE DEMONIC NATURE!***

KYLE AND ME AREN'T ***NUTS,*** Y'KNOW! ***WE SAW WHAT WE SAW!***

HEY!

CAN'T YOU ***CHUMPS*** TELL HE DOESN'T WANT YOU AROUND?! ***SCRAM!***

THAT RED-HEADED GIRL AND I WOULD SOON BECOME ***BEST FRIENDS.***

AS I WATCHED THE BRAVERMAN BOYS WALK UP TO HER, I FELT MY FACE GO HOT WITH ANGER.

CHECK IT OUT, KENNY! THIS ***MOUTHY GIRL*** IS STICKIN' UP FOR KENT!

THEY MUST BE ***LOVEBIRDS!***

SMOOCHIE! SMOOCHIE!

NO...
NOT AGAIN!
WHY ARE YOU DOING THIS TO ME AGAIN?!
I THREW YOU AWAY!

AS IF THEY UNDERSTOOD—
?!
—THE VOICES LEFT ME.

ALL OF IT LEFT ME.

YEOWCH!
WAP!

NOT TRYING TO BE MEAN, KID, BUT YOU'RE PRETTY TERRIBLE AT STICKING UP FOR YOURSELF.
HA HA. YOU'RE PROBABLY RIGHT.
THANKS FOR HANDLING THOSE JERKS.
I WAS FINALLY AN ORDINARY BOY.

MY DAD AND I JUST MOVED INTO TOWN.
CAME TO SERVICE HOPING TO MEET SOME FOLKS. MY NAME'S LANA LANG.
WELCOME TO SMALLVILLE, LANA. I'M CLARK KENT.
PERFECTLY ORDINARY.

PERFECT.
LOOK AT THIS. I LOVE BEING A PART OF THIS.
A PART OF THEM.
SON...

PLEASE DON'T CALL ME THAT.
I'M FROM A TOWN CALLED SMALLVILLE. I WAS RAISED BY JONATHAN AND MARTHA KENT.
THEY'RE MY PARENTS.

HOWEVER YOU'RE DOING THIS, HOWEVER YOU'RE APPEARING TO ME?
PLEASE.
STOP.

I'VE FINALLY CREATED A LIFE FOR MYSELF WHERE NO ONE LOOKS AT ME IN FEAR.
NO ONE WHO ISN'T COMMITTING A CRIME, ANYWAY.
PLEASE DON'T RUIN THAT FOR ME.
BUT DON'T YOU WANT THE TRUTH?

I WANT MY LIFE MORE.
GOODBYE.

ALL THIS TIME, I'VE REMEMBERED IT WRONG.
CAPTAIN DESMO, YOU FOOL!
I'VE BEEN A WEIRDO ALL ALONG, EVEN WITH MY OLD JACKET, EVEN IN CHINATOWN.
YOU AND YOUR PITIABLE PLANET DO NOT STAND A CHANCE AGAINST ME!
FOR I AM GENGHIS AHKIM THE INTERGALACTIC CONQUEROR!
YOU UNDERESTIMATE US EARTHLINGS AT YOUR OWN PERIL—
ALWAYS WATCHING FROM THE SIDELINES, ALWAYS LOOKING FOR SOME CLUE THAT MIGHT HELP ME FIT IN.
NEVER FINDING IT.
YOU ALIEN SCUM!

WE SHALL SEE ABOUT THAT, DESMO! MWHAHAHA!
EGADS! HE'S FLYING! RUN!
AIYEEE!

WHOA!
GENGHIS AHKIM CAN FLY?!
HOW'D THEY DO THAT?!
MOVIEMAKERS ARE SO CLEVER. THEY MUST'VE USED SOME SORT OF WIRING, RIGHT?

NO WAY A HUMAN BEING COULD DEFY GRAVITY LIKE THAT...
NO MATTER HOW STRONG OR FAST...

OR SUPER.
JUST LIKE THAT, A THEORY PIECES TOGETHER LIKE A PUZZLE IN MY MIND.
I HAVE TO TALK IT THROUGH WITH SOMEONE.

HEY, QUIT BLOCKING THE SCREEN!
WHERE'S TOMMY?
SORRY!

HOLD IT AS LIGHT AS YOU CAN, LIKE IT'S AN EGG THAT MIGHT CRACK.
GOT IT?
I THINK SO.

THEN LET 'ER RIP!

PAFF!

YEOW! YOU ALMOST BROKE MY OTHER HAND!
AW, JEEZ! I DIDN'T MEAN TO—
KIDDIN', CHUCK! BUT SERIOUSLY, THAT WAS WAAAY FASTER THAN BEFORE!
WHAT ARE YOU GUYS DOING OUT HERE?

EH. DIDN'T FEEL LIKE BEING STUCK IN A THEATER.
BUT THIS WAS *YOUR IDEA!*
SIS, HOW ARE WE SUPPOSED TO CONCENTRATE ON A DUMB *SPACE MOVIE* WHEN WE'VE GOT A *CHAMPIONSHIP GAME* COMING UP?
YOUR *CAST* IS GONNA MAKE IT HARD FOR YOU TO PITCH, TOMMY!
WHICH IS WHY I GOTTA TEACH CHUCK HOW TO THROW A PROPER FASTBALL!
WHY *HIM?!*
HE HELPED SAVE ME, DIDN'T HE?
HE DID. BUT YOU EVER WONDER HOW HE KNEW WHERE THE KLAN TOOK YOU?
HE WAS AT OUR HOUSE THAT NIGHT, TOMMY! WEARING A *HOOD!* HE WAS THE ONE WHO THREW THE *BOMB!*
I RECOGNIZED HIS *BOOTS!*
CHUCK...?
...
SHE'S RIGHT.
THAT WAS ME.
LISTEN, I AM *SO, SO SORRY.* I NEVER WANTED TO HURT YOUR FAMILY. I *SWEAR.*

I BELIEVE HIM.
WHAT?! ARE YOU SOFT IN THE NOGGIN?!

CHUCK HERE IS A NATURAL PITCHER, ALMOST AS NATURAL AS ME. YOU KNOW HOW BIG OUR WINDOW IS?
WAY BIGGER THAN THE STRIKE ZONE.
SO... YOU MISSED ON PURPOSE?

I DID. LIKE I SAID, I DIDN'T WANT TO HURT YOUR FAMILY. NOT YOU, NOT THE UNITY HOUSE.
I DON'T WANNA HURT ANYBODY.

HOW WERE YOU GONNA HURT THE UNITY HOUSE?
WHAT? I JUST SAID I DIDN'T WANNA HURT THE UNITY HOUSE!
THEN WHY EVEN BRING IT UP? SPILL, CHUCK! IS THAT WHY YOU WERE ALL NERVES BEFORE?
IS THAT WHY YOU SUGGESTED WE COME SEE A MOVIE YOU DIDN'T EVEN WANT TO SEE?

I...I...
HOW DID SUPERMAN PUT IT?
"IF YOU MIGHT BE ABLE TO HELP ANOTHER PERSON, YOU OUGHT TO AT LEAST TRY."

MY UNCLE IS THE GRAND SCORPION OF THE KLAN OF THE FIERY KROSS, OKAY?! HE'S THE ONE WHO BROUGHT ME TO THE MEETING IN THAT SPOT BY THE RIVER.
HIS NAME IS MATT RIGGS.
BUT YOU GOTTA UNDERSTAND, HE'S A GOOD GUY DEEP DOWN!
HE MIGHT BE WRONG ABOUT THIS, BUT HE'S BEEN THERE FOR MY MOM AND ME EVER SINCE WE LOST MY...
EVER SINCE WE NEEDED HIM.
NOW, I DON'T KNOW FOR SURE...BUT I'M WORRIED SOMETHING TERRIBLE MIGHT HAPPEN TO THE UNITY HOUSE.
EVEN IF IT DOES, THOUGH, IT'S OKAY, RIGHT? BECAUSE WE'RE ALL HERE NOW!
YOU IDIOT! THE KIDS ARE ALL HERE, BUT WHAT ABOUT REVEREND LEEDS, RABBI STONE, AND FATHER SHAIN?! DID YOU CHECK THEIR OFFICE?
I DIDN'T EVEN THINK ABOUT THAT...
THEN WE GOTTA GO BACK TO MAKE SURE!
JIMMY!
COME ON!

THE UNITY HOUSE.

AW, JEEZ.

AND LOOK! THE LIGHT IS ON IN THE CLERGY'S OFFICE!

WE CAN'T LET THOSE KLANSMEN GET AWAY! I'M GONNA TRY TO STALL 'EM, ***LOIS LANE-STYLE!***

WHENEVER SHE DOES IT, ***SUPERMAN*** SHOWS UP IN THE NICK OF TIME!

LET'S HOPE HE DOES THE SAME FOR ***ME!***

NOT THE BRIGHTEST PLAN, BUT I GUESS IT'S THE BEST WE'VE GOT!

ROBERTA, WHAT ARE YOU—?!

NO WAY I'M LETTING YOU FACE THOSE CREEPS ***ALONE! COME ON!***

YOU GUYS GET GOING ON THOSE PHONE CALLS!

SHAKE A LEG ALREADY!

EXCUSE ME, MISTER, UH—
WHO—?!
MR. BEDSHEET BIGOT.

JIMMY OLSEN, CUB REPORTER FOR THE *DAILY PLANET*. THIS IS MY ASSOCIATE *ROBERTA LEE*.
HELLO.
YOU *BRATS* DON'T KNOW WHO YOU'RE MESSING WITH!

OUTTA THE WAY!
WOULD YOU MIND ANSWERING A FEW QUESTIONS?

HERE. A LITTLE SOMETHING TO GET YOU THROUGH THE EVENING SLUMP.
Metro Cafe

IT'S NOT YOUR TURN.
I KNOW.
LOIS, ABOUT WHAT HAPPENED AT THE COFFEE SHOP... ***I'M SORRY.***

IF YOU'RE WILLING, I'D LOVE TO HEAR MORE ABOUT YOUR METROPOLIS HEALTH DEPARTMENT INVESTIGATION.
RING! RING!
HM.

LIKE I WAS SAYING EARLIER, I THINK THE HEALTH DEPARTMENT AND THE—
SLOW DOWN, YOUNG MAN. I CAN BARELY CATCH A WORD. WHAT'S THIS ABOUT THE ***UNITY HOUSE?***

THE UNITY HOUSE...?
CLARK, ARE YOU EVEN LISTENING?

HONESTLY, YOU'RE *IMPOSSIBLE!*
NO! LOIS, I-!
HANG ON.

I'LL PUT YOU THROUGH TO MR. WHITE.
THEY'LL HAVE TO CALL BACK.
LOOK WHO STEPPED OFF THE ELEVATOR.

PERRY WHITE! WHAT IS THIS?!
EXACTLY WHAT IT SAYS IT IS, INSPECTOR HENDERSON! WE'RE OFFERING A *REWARD* FOR THE KLAN!

I DON'T MEAN TO PRY, BUT DID I HEAR SOMETHING ABOUT THE *UNITY HOUSE?*
YOU DIDN'T CATCH HIS NAME, DID YOU?
THE CALLER WAS TALKING AWFULLY FAST. I'M SURE HE'LL CALL BACK IF IT'S IMPORTANT.

IT WAS *TOMMY LEE.*

FIRST QUESTION: WHAT EXACTLY IS THIS LOOK YOU'RE GOING FOR?
RACIST POINTY-HEADED GHOST?
RACIST UPSIDE-DOWN ICE CREAM CONE?
RACIST GIANT-SIZED DUNCE CAP?
WE GOT A QUESTION FOR YOU, KID.
WHY WOULD A GOOD 100 PERCENT AMERICAN LIKE YOU PAL AROUND WITH SOME CHING-CHONG?
YOUR MOM TAUGHT YOU NOT TO FEED STRAY DOGS, DIDN'T SHE? WHAT YOU'RE DOING AIN'T NO DIFFERENT!
YOU TAKE THAT BACK BEFORE I—
OW!
WAP!
ROBERTA!
THE CHING-CHONG WANTS TO GET VIOLENT, EH?!
WHY DON'T YOU TAKE OFF YOUR MASK AND CALL ME THAT TO MY FACE?!
YOU KNOW WHAT WE DO TO RABID DOGS HERE IN AMERICA?
WE PUT 'EM DOW—
GRK!

WHAT—?!
SUPERMAN!
WHAT WAS IT YOU CALLED THESE GOONS, ROBERTA?
OH, THAT'S RIGHT.
BIGOTS IN BEDSHEETS.
I KNEW YOU'D SHOW UP, SUPERMAN! I JUST KNEW IT!
YOU HAVE TO HURRY! WE THINK THEY HID A BOMB SOMEWHERE IN THE BUILDING!
YOU TWO GENIUSES DECIDED TO BOMB A CHILDREN'S COMMUNITY CENTER?!
THIS ISN'T A COMMUNITY CENTER, SUPERMAN! IT'S A THREAT TO THE PURITY OF AMERICA!
IF YOU TRULY LOVED YOUR NATION—AND YOUR RACE—YOU WOULD RECOGNIZE THAT!

GAH!
TOSS
I ONLY NEED ONE OF YOU TO FIND THAT BOMB.

D-DON'T LEAVE ME UP HERE!
I WOULDN'T SQUIRM TOO MUCH! WHO KNOWS HOW LONG THAT BRANCH WILL HOLD!

YOU KIDS KEEP A GOOD DISTANCE AWAY, IN CASE I DON'T DEFUSE THE BOMB IN TIME!
KRACK!

YOU'RE SUPERMAN! YOU'RE DEFINITELY GONNA—
GO! NOW!

NOW, I'LL BE FINE NO MATTER WHAT, BUT IF YOU DON'T TELL ME WHERE THAT BOMB IS, YOU'LL BE BLOWN TO BITS.
YOU'RE MAKING A BAD BET, SUPERMAN!
I'D RATHER DIE THAN TELL YOU ANYTHING! IN FACT, I'VE DREAMED OF BEING A MARTYR FOR MY RACE!
HELL, ONCE THEY CLEAN UP ALL THE FILTH IN THIS CITY, THEY'LL PROBABLY PUT UP A STATUE OF ME!
MUFFLED NOISES FROM UPSTAIRS.
RABBI STONE! FATHER SHAIN! REVEREND LEEDS!
GOD BLESS YOU, SUPERMAN!
ARE YOU THE ONLY ONES HERE?!
YES, I BELIEVE SO.

WHERE IS THAT BOMB? I CAN MAKE OUT A TICKING SOUND—
TICK TICK TICK...
—BUT IT'S THE CLOCK. THERE'S TICKING EVERYWHERE, ACTUALLY.
TICK TICK
A BUILDING FULL OF CLOCKS.
I NEED TO LOOK THROUGH, THE WAY I FOUND TOMMY.
I TRY TO HEAR THE VOICES AGAIN.
TICK
I TRY TO SMELL THAT GREEN CRYSTAL SMELL.
COME BACK.
PLEASE. I'M SORRY I WALKED AWAY FROM YOU! I NEED...
I NEED YOU RIGHT NOW! I NEED THE POWER TO LOOK THROUGH.
FATHER...? MOTHER...?
TICK
TICK
TIC
HA! IT'S TOO LATE, SUPERMAN, EVEN FOR YOU!
SWEET MARTYRDOM, HERE I COME!
RUMB
THE FLOOR TREMBLES.
RUMBLE

I HAVE NO CHOICE.
KROOOM!
I RUN.

LEAVE LAW ENFORCEMENT TO THE POLICE, PERRY! YOU DON'T SEE MY OFFICERS PUBLISHING NEWS ARTICLES, DO YOU?!
WHY CAN'T PRIVATE CITIZENS JOIN THE FIGHT FOR JUSTICE?! SUPERMAN'S NOT A COP! LOOK AT HIM!

JUST THIS MORNING, I SPOKE WITH A KID, PROBABLY THE LEAST CONVINCING LIAR I'VE EVER MET.

LONG STORY SHORT, I'VE NOW GOT A LEAD ON THE METROPOLIS KLAN'S MAIN GUY!
DING!

BUT WORD ON THE STREET IS, YOUR HEADLINE SPOOKED THE SUSPECT SO BADLY THAT HE'S GONE INTO HIDING!
W-WELL, THAT'S NOT WHAT I MEANT TO—
TRUST ME, "INSPECTOR."

ONE RACE! ONE COLOR! ONE RELIGION!
NO ONE IS HIDING FROM THE LIKES OF YOU!

HEY, HOW ABOUT WE SIT DOWN FOR AN INTERVIEW?
"INTERVIEW?" HA!
WHAT A THING TO ASK WHEN YOU'VE GOT A KNIFE IN YOUR FACE!
GET OVER THERE WITH THE REST OF 'EM!

FUNNY. DR. WILLIAM JENNINGS SPOKE IN THE EXACT SAME WAY.

I CAN'T TELL YOU HOW UNBEARABLE IT'S BEEN, WATCHING YOU STRUT AROUND TOWN WITH THAT BADGE PINNED TO YOUR CHEST, BOY!
HAND IT OVER!
OVER MY DEAD BODY.

FINE. HAVE IT YOUR WAY!
NO, DON'T DO IT! KILL HIM LIKE THAT AND HE DIES A COP!

HAND OVER THE BADGE, BOY, OR PERRY WHITE GETS IT!
NRF!

I COULDN'T SAVE THE UNITY HOUSE.
I'VE FAILED.

AM I DEAD...?
I MUST BE!
HA HA!
I STAYED TRUE TO THE VERY END, O LORD! I'M READY FOR MY REWARD!

EXCUSE ME. YOUR FOOT'S ON FIRE.
ACK! THERE ARE JEWS IN HEAVEN?!

NONE OF THIS WOULD HAVE HAPPENED IF MY FAMILY HAD NEVER COME TO METROPOLIS.
YOU CAN'T THINK LIKE THAT, ROBERTA! THIS IS THE KLAN'S FAULT AND NO ONE ELSE'S!

BESIDES, IF YOUR FAMILY HAD NEVER COME, I NEVER WOULD'VE MET YOU.
AND, UH, TOMMY.
YOU AND TOMMY, I MEAN.
JIMMY! MR. WOULD-BE MARTYR HERE BURNED HIMSELF PRETTY BADLY!
WE'LL HAVE TO STOP BY THE HOSPITAL ON OUR WAY TO THE JAILHOUSE! CAN YOU—
OH, MY FOOT! IT BUUURNS!
GIVE ROBERTA A RIDE HOME? YOU GOT IT, SUPERMAN!
YOU KNOW WHAT I'M WONDERING? WHEN THE KLAN SHOWED UP AT MY HOUSE, THERE WERE DOZENS OF THEM. HOW COME ONLY TWO CAME HERE?
MAYBE THE REST OF 'EM WERE BUSY.
BUSY WITH WHAT?
ATTACKING ANOTHER TARGET, MAYBE?
BUT WHAT OTHER TARGET IS—
!
!
WAIT! D-D-DON'T JUST LEAVE ME UP HERE!

GASP!
JIMMY...
OH NO...

CHAPTER 3

SMALLVILLE. 1936.
IN A TINY TOWN LIKE SMALLVILLE, A VISITING CIRCUS WAS A BIG DEAL.
WHICH IS WHY LANA INSISTED ON GOING.
AW, IT'S BARELY A DRIZZLE, CLARK! THIS'LL TOTALLY BE WORTH IT!
I HOPE SO, LANA.
NOT TO COMPLAIN, BUT I WAS SOAKED. I WASN'T LOOKING FORWARD TO WATCHING THE SHOW IN WET PANTS.

WE REALLY APPRECIATE YOU KIDS LETTING US TAG ALONG ON YOUR DATE!
OH, UM... MA, IT'S NOT A DATE.
CLARK AND I ARE BEST FRIENDS, IS ALL.
OF COURSE. BEST FRIENDS... JUST LIKE MARTHA AND ME.

I'M SURPRISED THIS MANY PEOPLE CAME OUT!
I'M TELLING YOU, FROM WHAT I REMEMBER AS A KID?
THE CIRCUS IS... IT'S...

IT'S LIKE THIS WHOLE OTHER WORLD INSIDE THAT TENT!
FULL OF FUN AND COLOR AND...AND...

WONDER!
YOU WANT WONDER, YOUNG LADY?
HOW ABOUT LETTING GO OF YOUR TICKET?

DESPITE THE GRUMPY GUY AT THE ENTRANCE, LANA WAS RIGHT.
IT WAS A WHOLE OTHER WORLD INSIDE.
THE ACROBATS, JUGGLERS, AND ANIMALS WEREN'T LIKE ANYTHING I'D EVER SEEN.
I FORGOT ALL ABOUT MY PANTS BEING SOAKED.
THE MOST INTRIGUING PERFORMER, THOUGH?
LADIEEES AND GENTLEMENNN! PLEASE PUT YOUR HANDS TOGETHER AND WELCOME TO THE CENTER RING A LIVING LEGEND!
A HERO OF MYTH!
THE STRONGEST STRONGMAN TO EVER WALK THE EARTH! I PRESENT TO YOU—

THE MIGHTY SAMSON!

CLAP! CLAP! CLAP!

HEY! IT'S THE GUY WHO TOOK OUR TICKETS!

WHAT? NO! THAT GUY WAS BALD! THIS GUY'S GOT LONGER HAIR THAN MINE!

LANA, HE'S CLEARLY WEARING A WIG!

WELL... IT'S NOT JUST THAT.

LOOK AT THE WAY HE CARRIES HIMSELF! AND THAT COSTUME!

YOU LIKE HIS COSTUME?! HE'S WEARING HIS UNDERWEAR ON THE OUTSIDE!

YEAH, BUT HE MAKES IT WORK SOMEHOW.

HUP— HUP—

OUTSIDE, THE RAIN HAD GROWN INTO A LIGHTNING STORM.
RUMBLE
RUMBLE

KRACK!!

GASP
IS THE TENT—?

FSS SS

FWOOOSH!
BVOOORRR!
AIYEEE!
RUN!

MOVE IT, FOLKS!
BVOOORRR!
LANA, CAN YOU MAKE SURE MY PARENTS ARE SAFE?
I GOTTA GO HELP!
BUT, CLARK—!
LET HIM GO, LANA! WHEN HE GETS LIKE THAT, THERE'S NO STOPPING HIM!
OY GEVALT!
RUN, GIRL! RUN!
GRRR...
YEOW!
ROARRR!
MMMRPH!

ROARRR!
YOU ALL RIGHT, MR. SAMSON?!
?!

LATER.
THANKS FOR THE POP.
A BOTTLE OF POP FOR SAVING MY *LIFE?*

DEAL OF THE *CENTURY,* KID!
Y'KNOW, THEY CALL *ME* THE WORLD'S STRONGEST STRONGMAN, BUT *YOU—*
CLINK

I'VE NEVER MET ANYBODY LIKE *YOU.*
YOU GOT A *REAL FUTURE* IN THE CIRCUS, KID! EVER PERFORMED IN FRONT OF PEOPLE?
NO.

I'VE ALWAYS BEEN AFRAID THAT IF PEOPLE SAW WHAT I COULD DO...I'D *SCARE* THEM.

HA! I HAD THE SAME PROBLEM! KNOW HOW I SOLVED IT?
A COSTUME.
THE MORE *COLORFUL,* THE BETTER!

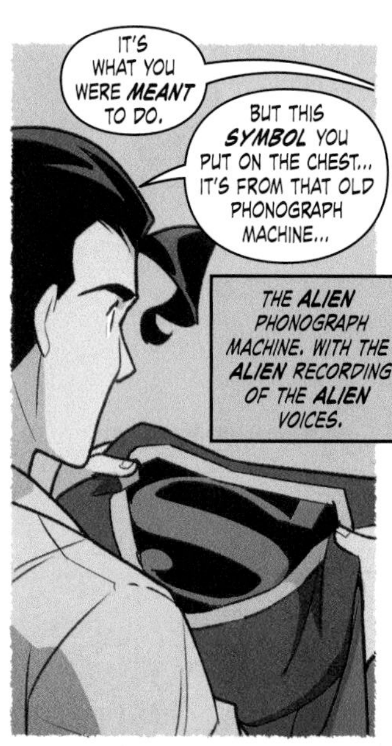

AND SO I BECAME A STRONGMAN, JUST LIKE THE ONES THEY HAVE AT THE CIRCUS, ONLY I HELP PEOPLE.

I WAS MAYBE EVEN THE WORLD'S STRONGEST STRONGMAN.

BUT STILL A HUMAN STRONGMAN.
TO EVERYONE ELSE, AT LEAST.
METROPOLIS. 1946.
GREAT SCOTT!
NFF!

LOOK! SUPERMAN'S ALREADY HERE!
WHAT'S HE DOING?!

HE MUST BE CLIMBING UP TO THE DAILY PLANET OFFICES!

BUT CLIMBING IS SO SLOW!
WHAT—?
WHAT CHOICE DOES HE HAVE, ROBERTA?
THE NEWSROOMS ARE ON THE 38TH FLOOR! IT'S NOT LIKE HE CAN FLY!
I DON'T KNOW...

JIMMY!
DUCK!
VROOOM!

THE KLAN.

THERE MIGHT BE PEOPLE IN THAT BUILDING WHO NEED OUR HELP!
LET'S GO!

NO ONE'S UP HERE.
HWOOOSH!

SUPERMAN!
IS EVERYONE ALL RIGHT?!
IT WAS HORRIBLE!
THOSE HOODED THUGS BURST IN AND TIED US UP!
WE THOUGHT WE'D BE STUCK HERE ALL NIGHT—

—UNTIL JIMMY AND HIS FRIEND CAME TO OUR RESCUE!
JIMMY! ROBERTA! WHAT ARE YOU TWO DOING HERE?!
HELPING YOU STOP THOSE BIGOTS!

THEY TOOK HOSTAGES WITH 'EM, SUPERMAN!
THEY GOT PERRY, LOIS, AND INSPECTOR HENDERSON!
ANY IDEA WHERE THEY'RE HEADED?

NO, I'M SORRY.
ACTUALLY, SUPERMAN, COME LOOK AT THIS!

THAT LIPSTICK HAS TO BE MS. LANE'S, RIGHT? I THINK SHE LEFT US A MESSAGE!
I CAN BARELY MAKE IT OUT! I'M IMPRESSED YOU EVEN FOUND THIS, ROBERTA!
I THOUGHT TO MYSELF, WHAT WOULD I DO IF I WERE STUCK IN LOIS LANE'S SITUATION?
I'D LEAVE BEHIND A CLUE OF SOME SORT.

W.J...
CALL IT A HUNCH, BUT THOSE ARE THE INITIALS OF MY DAD'S CO-WORKER WILLIAM JENNINGS.
WHEN HE VISITED MY FAMILY, HE CAME OFF LIKE A REAL CREEP.

A KLANNISH SORT OF CREEP?
WOULDN'T BE SURPRISED.
IT'S WORTH CHECKING OUT.

JIMMY, ALL RIGHT IF I BORROW THE OFFICE PHONE BOOK? I NEED TO LOOK UP JENNINGS'S ADDRESS!
WAY AHEAD OF YOU, SUPERMAN!

HWOOOOSH!

THE UNITY HOUSE.
HOLY-!
WHERE'S ROBERTA?!

EXCUSE ME, MR. FIREMAN? HAVE YOU SEEN MY SISTER? CHINESE GIRL IN A RED SUPERMAN JACKET?
IS SHE FRIENDS WITH THAT JIMMY OLSEN KID FROM THE DAILY PLANET?
YEAH, THAT'S HER!

DON'T WORRY, YOUNG MAN. SHE WASN'T HURT. THANKS TO SUPERMAN, NOBODY WAS. I THINK JIMMY TOOK HER HOME.
YOU BOYS LOOK LIKE YOU'VE BEEN THROUGH THE WRINGER. WHY DON'T YOU HEAD HOME YOURSELVES?

HEY, TOMMY...?
I'VE BEEN THINKING...WHAT HAPPENED TO THE UNITY HOUSE WAS ABSOLUTELY WRONG, OF COURSE.
BUT...IS IT REALLY ALL THAT BAD TO WANT TO LIVE AROUND ONLY PEOPLE WHO LOOK LIKE YOU?
WAIT. WHAT ARE YOU SAYING, CHUCK?
I...I DON'T KNOW! I'M JUST TRYING TO MAKE SENSE OF IT ALL!

A BROKEN ARM'S NOT ENOUGH?! YOU WANT ME TO QUIT THE TEAM?!
NO, NO! THAT'S NOT—!
YOU WANT MY FAMILY TO MOVE BACK TO CHINATOWN, IS THAT IT?!
I...I...!
SPIT IT OUT!
I WANT TO KNOW THAT MY FAMILY'S NOT EVIL!
...
BACK IN CHINATOWN, THE ONLY BASEBALL I EVER GOT TO PLAY WAS PICKUP.
THE UNITY HOUSE IS THE FIRST TEAM I'VE BEEN ON WHERE ALL THE PLAYERS WEAR MATCHING CAPS AND JERSEYS! A REAL TEAM, Y'KNOW?
SURE, I HAVEN'T GOTTEN TO PLAY AN ACTUAL GAME WITH YOU GUYS. AND NOW THAT I'M HURT, IT'LL BE A GOOD LONG WHILE BEFORE I DO.
BUT THAT'S WHY I TAUGHT YOU THAT FASTBALL, RIGHT? I STILL WANT US TO WIN!
I THOUGHT WE WERE ON THE SAME TEAM, CHUCK. ARE YOU SAYING WE'RE NOT?
TOMMY... I...I DON'T KNOW WHAT I'M SAYING.
WHATEVER.
I'LL SEE YOU AROUND.

ELSEWHERE IN METROPOLIS.
YOU CLOWNS MUST'VE DRESSED UP IN YOUR NIGHT-GOWNS FOR A REASON! WHAT DO YOU WANT?!
WE'RE GOING TO TEACH THE DAILY PLANET A LESSON ABOUT INTERFERING WITH KLAN BUSINESS!
BECAUSE OF RATS LIKE YOU, GOOD, HONEST, ONE HUNDRED PERCENT AMERICANS HAVE TO WEAR HOODS OVER OUR FACES JUST TO SAY WHAT WE REALLY BELIEVE!
LISTEN. I'M THE ONE YOU REALLY HATE, AREN'T I?
SO HOW ABOUT YOU LET MR. WHITE AND MS. LANE GO?
YOU'RE NOT WEARING YOUR BADGE ANYMORE, BOY! NO NEED TO PLAY HERO!
INSPECTOR HENDERSON ISN'T A HERO BECAUSE OF HIS BADGE, YOU IMBECILE!
LET THEM GO AND YOU CAN DO WHAT YOU WANT WITH ME!
OH, WE'RE GOING TO DO WHAT WE WANT WITH YOU REGARDLESS!
SHING!
THE LOYAL KNIGHT WHO GIFTED ME THIS BLADE TOLD ME ALL ABOUT ITS STORIED PAST!
IT'S BEEN USED IN THE RITUALS OF THE KLAN OF THE FIERY KROSS FOR GENERATIONS!

YOU QUIT YOUR LAUGHING, BOY!

AS SOON AS YOU FELLAS QUIT ACTING *LAUGHABLE,* I'LL QUIT *LAUGHING.*

THAT'S IT!

I'M GONNA ***CUT*** THE LAUGHTER RIGHT ***OUT OF YOU!***

SMASH!

SUPERMAN!

IF YOU'RE SMART, YOU'LL SURRENDER IMMEDIATELY!
NEVER!
SHATTER!
MY SWORD!
WELL, YOU GET WHAT YO PAY FOR.
YAAA-
WAP!
YEOWCH!
Y-Y-YOU'RE NOT GONNA PUNCH ME BACK, ARE YOU...?
PLEEEASE DON'T PUNCH ME BACK!
I WON'T PUNCH YOU.
IF I DID, I'D PROBABLY KILL YOU.

flick.
KRASH!
!
KLINK!
KLINK!
PERRY! INSPECTOR! HOLD STILL SO I CAN CUT YOU OUT OF THAT ROPE!
KNIGHTS, IF WE ALL WORK TOGETHER, WE CAN HANDLE HIM!
DOUBT IT.

TAKE HIM DOWN!
WHOA!
WHIRL!
YIKES!
GAH!
KRASH!
HELP! I'M ON FIRE! HELP MEEE!
HANG ON!
FWOOOSH!

I'M BURNINGGG!
PAT!
PAT!
STOP MOVING AROUND SO MUCH!

WE GOTTA PUT THIS FIRE OUT!
POW!
USE THIS!

HUH...?
GET OFFA ME! DON'T TOUCH ME!
FUNNY WAY OF SHOWING GRATITUDE, MISTER!
STOMP!
STOMP!

YOU EXPECT ME TO BE GRATEFUL FOR GETTING CONTAMINATED BY YOU?!
YOU OUGHTTA BE PUNISHED!

YOU NO-GOOD, FILTHY—
DROP THAT THING BEFORE YOU PUT SOMEBODY'S EYE OUT!

SMACK!
I SAID DROP IT!

INSPECTOR, I FOUND THIS ON THE GROUND. IT GOT PRETTY **BANGED UP.**

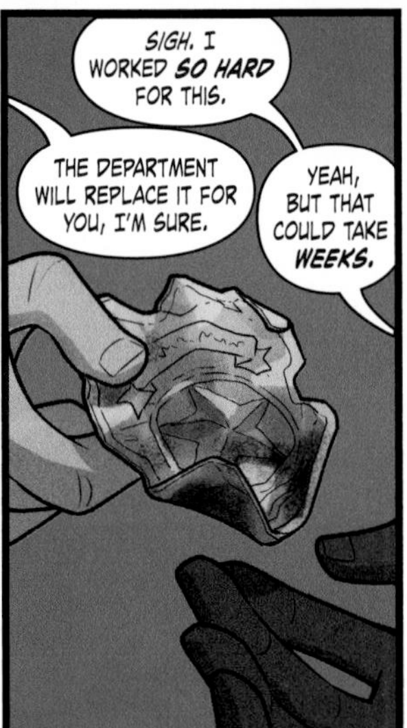
SIGH. I WORKED **SO HARD** FOR THIS.
THE DEPARTMENT WILL REPLACE IT FOR YOU, I'M SURE.
YEAH, BUT THAT COULD TAKE **WEEKS.**

IT'S JUST A **BADGE,** INSPECTOR. IT'S NOT WHAT MAKES YOU A **POLICE OFFICER!**
UNFORTUNATELY, NOT EVERYONE IN METROPOLIS SEES IT THAT WAY, MR. WHITE.

ROBERTA, JIMMY; DON'T GET ME WRONG. I'M NOT CONDONING YOU TWO PUTTING YOURSELVES IN DANGER...
BUT *THANK YOU.*
I TOLD YOU WE'D HELP YOU STOP THOSE BIGOTS, SUPERMAN!
YEAH...

I'VE HALF A MIND TO—
TO WHAT, SUPERMAN? PUNCH ME? KILL ME? GO AHEAD!
KILL ME AND I PROMISE YOU, A HUNDRED MEN EXACTLY LIKE ME WILL RISE UP TO TAKE MY PLACE!
THEN I'LL BRING A HUNDRED OF THEM TO JUSTICE!
YOU DON'T SEEM TO UNDERSTAND THAT THE KLAN OF THE FIERY KROSS ISN'T JUST A GROUP OF MEN. WE ARE A CONVICTION—
THE CONVICTION THAT A STRONG AMERICA IS A PURE AMERICA!
AND EVEN YOU CAN'T SMASH THAT WITH YOUR FISTS!
WHEN PUSH COMES TO SHOVE, YOU CANNOT UNITE A NATION OF PEOPLE WHO SHARE NEITHER BLOOD NOR HISTORY!
AND AS MUCH AS YOU WANT TO DENY IT, SUPERMAN, YOU ARE ONE OF US!
I'M NOT ONE OF YOU! I'M NOTHING LIKE YOU!
TELL ME, HOW DID YOU BECOME WHAT YOU ARE? WAS IT MYSTIC TRAINING, LIKE THE RUMORS SAY? A MEGAVITAMIN SERUM?
THE TRUTH IS, WHATEVER YOU DID WOULDN'T HAVE WORKED HAD YOU BEEN OF INFERIOR BLOOD!
THAT'S WHY MY NEPHEW ADMIRES YOU SO MUCH, ISN'T IT? THAT'S WHY THE WHOLE COUNTRY ADMIRES YOU!
YOU'RE LIVING PROOF OF JUST HOW SUPERIOR A WHITE MAN CAN BE!
GET IN THE TRUCK.
SHOVE!

HWOOOSH!

DON'T WORRY, GRAND SCORPION. I'LL HAVE YOU OUT OF HERE IN NO TIME!

ONE RACE! ONE COLOR! ONE RELIGION!

MY GOOD AND LOYAL KNIGHT!

THANK YOU FOR THE RIDE, SUPERMAN.
YOU'RE NOT FEELING SICK?
I'M OKAY. I APPRECIATE YOU SOFTENING THE LANDING OF YOUR LEAP.
UM...SUPERMAN?
THIS MIGHT BE COMPLETELY OUT OF TURN, BUT...
CAN I ASK YOU SOMETHING?
OF COURSE.
WHEN YOU DO THAT...WHEN YOU SOFTEN YOUR LANDING BY ACTUALLY DEFYING GRAVITY...IS IT STILL CALLED LEAPING? ISN'T IT MORE LIKE...
FLYING?
I-I-
I'M NOT SURE WHAT YOU'RE GETTING AT, ROBERTA!
MAYBE YOU'RE NOT EVEN DOING IT CONSCIOUSLY...AND I DEFINITELY WOULDN'T HAVE NOTICED IF I DIDN'T HAVE SUCH A GURGLY STOMACH.
BUT YOU'RE... LIMITING YOURSELF!
I COULD FEEL IT!
WH-WHAT-?!
I'VE THOUGHT AND THOUGHT ABOUT WHY.
I HAVE A THEORY.
...
CAN I SAY IT?
GO ON.
YOU WANT TO FIT IN BETTER.

YOU WANT EVERYBODY TO BELIEVE THAT YOU'RE JUST A BETTER VERSION OF A NORMAL HUMAN.

HUMANS RUN. YOU JUST RUN FASTER. HUMANS JUMP. YOU JUST JUMP HIGHER. HUMANS LIFT STUFF. YOU JUST LIFT HEAVIER STUFF.

BUT THE TRUTH IS... YOU CAN DO THINGS THAT ARE ENTIRELY DIFFERENT FROM WHAT HUMANS CAN DO...

RIGHT?

LIKE FLY!

AND YOU HOLD BACK BECAUSE YOU'RE AFRAID THAT IF PEOPLE FIND OUT, THEY'LL STOP CALLING YOU SUPERMAN. INSTEAD, THEY'LL CALL YOU SUPER...

SUPER SOMETHING ELSE.

TO BE HONEST, I'VE TRIED NOT TO GIVE ANY OF THAT MUCH THOUGHT.

AFTER ALL, MINDING YOURSELF TOO MUCH IS A GOOD WAY TO LOSE YOUR MIND.

BUT YOU GOTTA MIND YOURSELF A LITTLE! DON'T YOU SEE, SUPERMAN?

YOU HOLDING BACK ACTUALLY ENDANGERS PEOPLE!

HWOOOSH!

LUTHERAN CHURCH
SMALLVI
LUTHERA
CHURCH
THIS WEEK
LEV 19:34
HWOOOSH!

KENT
CLARK?! WHAT ARE YOU DOING HERE?!
WHAT'S WRONG?!

I...I NEED TO KNOW THAT NO MATTER WHAT HAPPENS, NO MATTER WHAT I MIGHT FIND OUT, NOTHING CHANGES BETWEEN US.
PROMISE ME WE'LL ALWAYS BE A FAMILY.

OH, SON...
WE MADE THAT PROMISE THE MOMENT WE LAID EYES ON YOU.

HWOoOSH!

ake Solitude
SPLASH!

HELLO, SON.

METROPOLIS. JUST BEFORE DAYBREAK.
HUFF! HUFF!
IT'S ME, MATTHEW RIGGS! THE GRAND SCORPION!
LET ME IN!
KNOCK! KNOCK!
HE WILL SEE YOU NOW.
THANK YOU, MY FELLOW KNIGHT!
GRAND IMPERIAL MOGUL! FORGIVE ME FOR COMING TO YOUR HEADQUARTERS ON SUCH SHORT NOTICE, BUT IT'S AN EMERGENCY!
MY FELLOW KNIGHTS HAVE ALL BEEN ARRESTED! I'M THE ONLY ONE WHO ESCAPED!
HELP US, GRAND IMPERIAL MOGUL! THE METROPOLIS CHAPTER OF THE KLAN OF THE FIERY KROSS IS IN TERRIBLE DANGER!
PLEASE, YOU MUST SEND FOR—
YES, GRAND SCORPION, THE METROPOLIS KLAN IS IN DANGER—

–BECAUSE OF YOUR ILL-CONSIDERED ACTIONS!
WHAT POSSESSED YOU TO LAUNCH AN ATTACK ON THE CITY'S MOST PROMINENT NEWSPAPER?!
THOSE SCOUNDRELS AT THE DAILY PLANET THREATENED US FIRST, DR. WILSON! THEY NEEDED A LESSON! IF SUPERMAN HADN'T SPOILED THINGS–
SUPERMAN?! SO IN ADDITION TO THE POLICE, YOU'VE GOT SUPERMAN HUNTING FOR US?!
ALL THIS BAD PUBLICITY, JUST WHEN WE'RE ABOUT TO LAUNCH A NEW MEMBERSHIP DRIVE!
THEY WOULD HAVE PAID US ONE HUNDRED DOLLARS EACH FOR INITIATION FEES! AND ANOTHER 25 DOLLARS FOR ROBES AND HOODS!
YOU'VE COST US THOUSANDS UPON THOUSANDS OF DOLLARS, RIGGS!
BUT, SIR, WHAT'S MONEY GOT TO DO WITH ANYTHING?!
FOOL!
SLAP!

WOW! JOOK? SALTED EGGS? PORK SUNG?
WE HAVEN'T HAD A BREAKFAST LIKE THIS IN AGES!
WE'RE CELEBRATING, CHILDREN!

LOOK AT THIS MORNING'S HEADLINE!
Daily Planet
KLAN OF THE FIERY KROSS ARRESTED

AND THAT'S NOT ALL! I QUIT MY JOB AT THE HEALTH DEPARTMENT YESTERDAY! IT TOOK ME THREE TRIES, BUT I FINALLY DID IT!
WAIT. WE'RE SUPPOSED TO BE HAPPY ABOUT THAT?
OF COURSE! YOUR FATHER NO LONGER BELIEVES IN THE DEPARTMENT'S MISSION!
MA, WHAT'S THAT SUPPOSED TO MEAN? WHAT'S THE MISSION—

SO...WE'RE MOVING BACK TO CHINATOWN, THEN?
NO, NO. WE'RE STAYING.
I'LL START MY JOB SEARCH IN EARNEST ON MONDAY.

BETWEEN THE TWO OF US, WE'LL HANDLE IT.
BUT FOR NOW, BREAKFAST!
RINGGG!
SOMEONE'S AT THE DOOR!

MS. LANE!
GOOD MORNING, ROBERTA!
JIMMY TOLD ME YOU WERE THE ONE WHO FIGURED OUT MY LIPSTICK MESSAGE.
I BROUGHT YOU A TOKEN OF *APPRECIATION.*

A PEN!
IN THE HANDS OF THE RIGHT PERSON, A PEN CAN BECOME *THE MOST POWERFUL INSTRUMENT* IN THE WORLD.
IT LOOKS SO *EXPENSIVE!*

THANK YOU!
IF YOU'RE EVER INTERESTED IN A CAREER IN *JOURNALISM,* COME BY MY OFFICE.
THE DAILY PLANET COULD ALWAYS USE *ANOTHER CUB REPORTER.*

I MIGHT TAKE YOU UP ON THAT, MS. LANE. ESPECIALLY IF MY DAD CAN'T FIND A JOB.
DR. LEE LEFT HIS POSITION AT THE METROPOLIS HEALTH DEPARTMENT? *INTERESTING.* ANY IDEA WHY?

I DON'T KNOW...MY MOM MENTIONED SOMETHING ABOUT THE DEPARTMENT'S *MISSION...*
HM. SOUNDS LIKE YOUR *FIRST LEAD* RIGHT THERE, ROBERTA!

"—A PLANET CALLED ***KRYPTON.***

"IN SOME WAYS, OUR PEOPLE WERE COMPLETELY ***DIFFERENT*** FROM THE PEOPLE OF EARTH.

"IN OTHER WAYS, WE WERE VERY MUCH THE ***SAME.***"

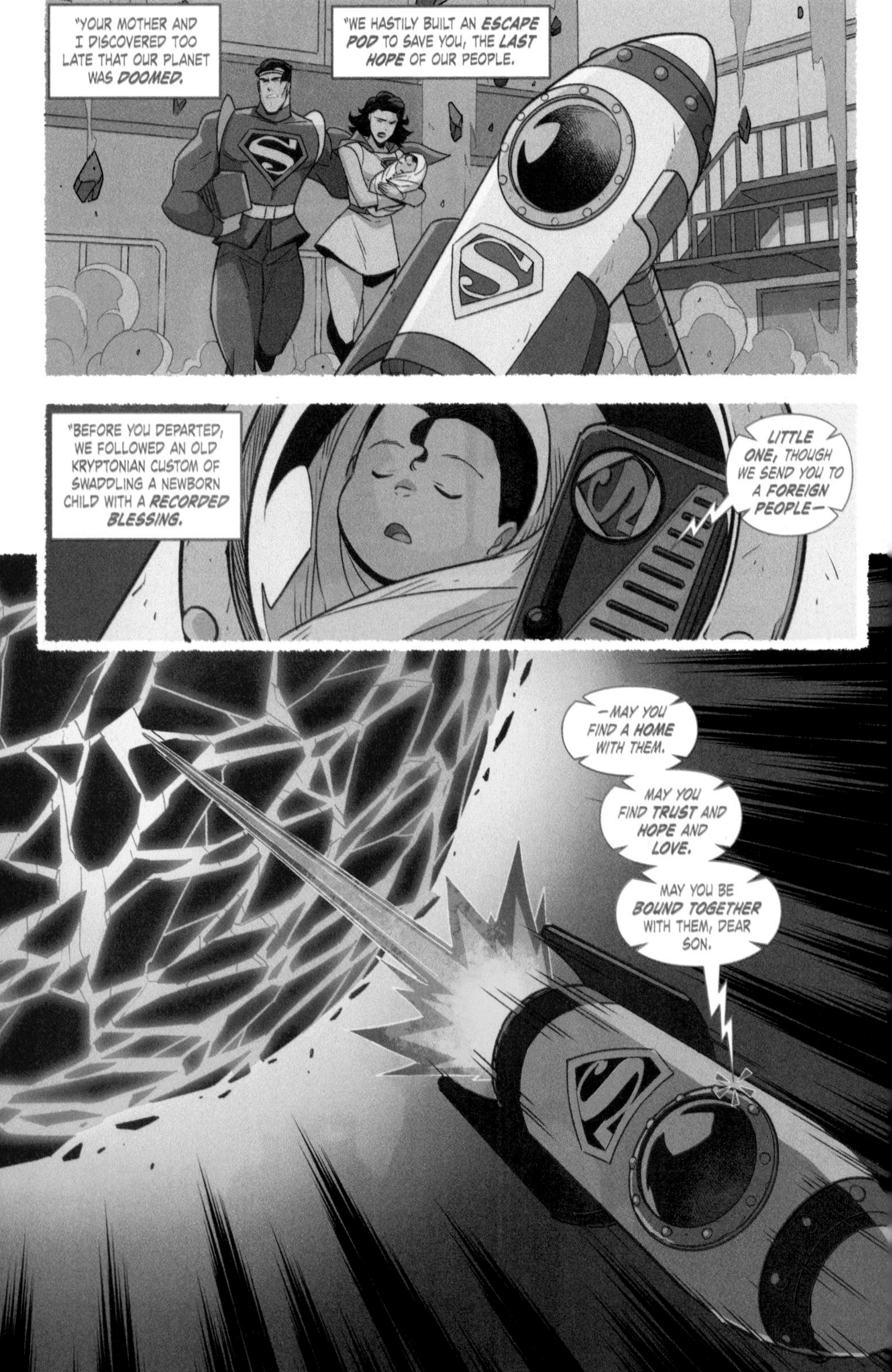
"YOUR MOTHER AND I DISCOVERED TOO LATE THAT OUR PLANET WAS DOOMED.
"WE HASTILY BUILT AN ESCAPE POD TO SAVE YOU, THE LAST HOPE OF OUR PEOPLE.
"BEFORE YOU DEPARTED, WE FOLLOWED AN OLD KRYPTONIAN CUSTOM OF SWADDLING A NEWBORN CHILD WITH A RECORDED BLESSING.
LITTLE ONE, THOUGH WE SEND YOU TO A FOREIGN PEOPLE—
—MAY YOU FIND A HOME WITH THEM.
MAY YOU FIND TRUST AND HOPE AND LOVE.
MAY YOU BE BOUND TOGETHER WITH THEM, DEAR SON.

MAY YOUR **TOMORROW** AND THEIRS BE **ONE.**

WAAAUUHH

OUR BLESSING CAME **TRUE,** KAL-EL.

YOU FOUND A **HOME.**

YOU TOLD US BEFORE THAT YOU LOVE BEING PART OF **THEM.**

YOU **ARE** A PART OF THEM, SON, AND YOU **ALWAYS** WILL BE.

BUT YOU'LL **ALWAYS** BE PART OF **US**, TOO.

MY **FIRST LEAD** ON A STORY, LOIS LANE SAID.
IT TOOK ME **ALL MORNING** TO FIND THE BOX OF STUFF THAT DAD HAD BROUGHT HOME FROM THE HEALTH DEPARTMENT.
HE'D HIDDEN IT IN AN OLD SUITCASE IN THE BASEMENT.

INSIDE ARE WEIRD-LOOKING GADGETS...

A **ROUND CASE** THAT'S HEAVIER THAN IT LOOKS...

AND MY FATHER'S **JOURNAL.**

AS I READ, I LEARN THE TRUTH ABOUT THE **METROPOLIS HEALTH DEPARTMENT.**
IT WAS FOUNDED BY **DR. SEGRET WILSON—**

—A MAN WHO ISN'T WHAT HE SEEMS.
TELL ME, RIGGS, WHAT HAVE YOU BEEN DOING WITH THE 25 PERCENT CUT YOU GET FROM OUR NEW RECRUITS' INITIATION FEES? THE TEN PERCENT CUT ON THEIR ROBES?
GIVING IT TO CHARITY?
OF COURSE NOT! BUT WE'RE NOT IN THIS FOR THE MONEY! WE ARE PURIFYING AMERICA!

WAIT A MINUTE. IS IT POSSIBLE YOU ACTUALLY BELIEVE ALL THAT "ONE RACE, ONE RELIGION, ONE COLOR" ROT?
"ROT"?! IT'S THE ABSOLUTE TRUTH!

TSK TSK. YOU'VE GOTTEN DRUNK ON THE SLOP WE PUT OUT FOR THE LITTLE NOBODIES WHO WANT TO BELIEVE THAT SOME OTHER RACE IS INFERIOR SO THEY CAN FEEL SUPERIOR!
RIGGS, WE ARE A BUSINESS THAT DEALS IN THE WORLD'S OLDEST COMMODITY: HATE!
AND WE DO IT TO FUND A DEFENSE PROGRAM AGAINST AN ACTUAL THREAT!

COME. LET ME SHOW YOU WHAT THE KLAN IS REALLY ABOUT.

IT'S FINE FOR ALL THESE FOREIGNERS TO COME TO AMERICA, SO LONG AS THEY KNOW THEIR ROLE!
TAKE DR. LEE, FOR EXAMPLE... HE PUT ON HIS LAB COAT AND DID AS HE WAS TOLD!
BECAUSE OF FOREIGNERS LIKE HIM, I CAN LIVE AS I DESERVE!
$2.79
$2.79
$3.99
$3.99
2 for $3

BUT EVERY NOW AND THEN, SOMEONE COMES ALONG WITH THE POWER TO BREAK OUT OF THEIR ROLE. I FOUNDED THE METROPOLIS HEALTH DEPARTMENT TO GUARD AGAINST THE SINGLE GREATEST THREAT TO PEOPLE LIKE ME...
SUPERMAN!

SURE, HE PASSES HIMSELF OFF AS A BOY SCOUT FOR NOW, BUT WHAT IF SOMEDAY HE TRADES HIS CAPE FOR A CROWN?
UNLIKE DR. LEE, WHO CAN ALWAYS BE CONTROLLED BY OUR KLAN MINIONS, SUPERMAN HAS REAL POWER!
I SPENT YEARS RESEARCHING A WAY TO DESTROY HIM, AND NOW I'VE FINALLY GOT IT!
S-SIR, WHO IS THAT MAN IN THE TANK?!
WHY, HE IS THE KEY TO OUR MISSION!
FROM HIS SECRET CONTACTS IN GERMANY, DR. WILSON LEARNED THAT THE NAZIS HAD IN THEIR POSSESSION A RARE SPACE ROCK THAT COULD BE HARNESSED FOR ENERGY.
THEY CALLED THIS ROCK DER GRÜNSTEIN—THE GREEN STONE.
FOR YEARS, DR. WILSON TRIED TO SECURE A PIECE OF DER GRÜNSTEIN.

HIS BIG BREAK CAME SHORTLY BEFORE MY FATHER BEGAN WORKING FOR HIM.
A NAZI SOLDIER CODE-NAMED THE ATOM MAN HAD MADE HIS WAY TO METROPOLIS.
BAM!
THE NAZIS HAD INFUSED THE ATOM MAN'S BLOOD...WITH DER GRÜNSTEIN, GIVING HIM SUPERMAN- LIKE POWERS.
DR. WILSON OBSERVED THE ATOM MAN'S BATTLE WITH SUPERMAN IN SECRET. WHAT HE SAW ASTOUNDED HIM.
THE ATOM MAN DIDN'T STAND A CHANCE, BUT EXPOSURE TO DER GRÜNSTEIN SEEMED TO WEAKEN SUPERMAN!
DR. WILSON ARRANGED FOR THE ATOM MAN TO BE TRANSFERRED FROM THE POLICE DEPARTMENT...TO THE METROPOLIS HEALTH DEPARTMENT.
HE, MY FATHER, AND JENNINGS USED BACTERIA TO EXTRACT DER GRÜNSTEIN FROM THE ATOM MAN'S BLOOD.
THEN WE PUT THE NAZI'S SPACE ROCK INTO WEAPONRY SPECIFICALLY DESIGNED TO DESTROY SUPERMAN!

IT'S SO HEAVY!
IT HAS TO BE! THE ONLY ELEMENT THAT CAN CONTAIN DER GRÜNSTEIN'S RADIATION—
—IS LEAD.
THIS CASE IS SO HEAVY BECAUSE IT'S MADE OF LEAD.
!
SO THAT'S WHY DAD LEFT HIS JOB. HE STOPPED BELIEVING IN THE DEPARTMENT'S MISSION.
AFTER MEETING SUPERMAN, DAD NO LONGER SAW HIM AS A THREAT.

YOU WANT TO KNOW MY THEORY ABOUT SUPERMAN, RIGGS? HE'S VULNERABLE TO A ROCK FROM OUTER SPACE BECAUSE HE IS FROM OUTER SPACE!
HOW... HOW CAN THAT BE?!
ALL THIS TIME, YOU'VE BEEN AFRAID OF THE WRONG KIND OF ALIEN! HA HA!
YOU STUPID, STUPID FOOL! YOU THINK THE WORLD IS DIVIDED BY RACE, BUT REALLY, IT'S DIVIDED BY POWER!
I HAVE POWER! AND YOU DO NOT!
OUR SKIN MAY BE THE SAME COLOR, BUT YOU AND I ARE NOTHING ALIKE!
YOU ARE AN INSECT! I AM A GOD!
VVVRRR...
DR. WILSON! WHAT ARE YOU DOING?!
I CAN'T HAVE A BLOODTHIRSTY FANATIC ENDANGERING MY REVENUE STREAM!
GOODBYE, GRAND SCORPION!
BRAAAK!
YOU TRAITOR!
WHAT?! LET GO!
YOU'RE A MISERABLE TRAITOR TO YOUR OWN KIND, WILSON!
HGK!

WELCOME EVERYBODY, TO METROPOLIS PARK! ARE WE IN FOR A TREAT!
TODAY, THE UNITY HOUSE OF METROPOLIS TAKES ON THE GOTHAM CITY BOYS' CLUB FOR THE DELAWARE BAY YOUTH LEAGUE CHAMPIONSHIP!
PLEASE BE GENEROUS AT THE CONCESSION STAND!
ALL PROCEEDS WILL BE DONATED TO THE RESTORATION OF THE UNITY HOUSE!
HOORAY!
THIS MIGHT BE THE FIRST BASEBALL GAME I'VE HAD TO DRAG YOU TO! WHAT'S GOING ON, TOMMY? ARE YOU GETTING SICK OR SOMETHING?
NAH.
JUST FIGURED THERE ARE BETTER WAYS TO SPEND A SATURDAY.
SINCE WHEN DID YOU BECOME SUCH A BASEBALL FAN, SIS?

HEY, LEES! OVER HERE!

I GOT COTTON CANDY!

AH. GOTCHA.

COME SIT WITH US, ROBERTA!

MAYBE I'LL NEVER BE BEST FRIENDS WITH THE UNITY HOUSE GIRLS.

GOOD AFTERNOON, DR. LEE, MRS. LEE!
INSPECTOR HENDERSON! I MUST CONFESS, WE NEVER PROPERLY ***THANKED*** YOU AND YOUR FRIENDS FOR COMING TO OUR AID ON THAT ***HORRIBLE NIGHT.***

COME HERE!
LET GO OF ME!

LET GO!
R111P!

YOU'RE NOT GETTING AWAY THAT EASILY, YOU FILTHY CHING-CHONG!
MMMPH!

THE CROWD GOES QUIET AS UNITY HOUSE STARTING PITCHER CHUCK RIGGS GETS READY TO THROW THE FIRST PITCH OF THE GAME!

BRAAAK!

ONE RACE! ONE COLOR! ONE RELIGION!
LET GO OF ME, YOU CREEP!
UNCLE MATT—?!
PEOPLE OF METROPOLIS...
I AM THE GRAND SCORPION OF THE KLAN OF THE FIERY KROSS!
BY YOUR VERY PRESENCE HERE, YOU ARE SUPPORTING THE SO-CALLED UNITY HOUSE—THAT BLIGHTED SYMBOL OF METROPOLIS'S FESTERING IMPURITY!
IS THAT REALLY WHAT YOU WANT?! DO YOU REALLY WANT YOUR CITY—
OUR NATION—TO COME APART AT THE SEAMS?!
HE'S GOT ROBERTA!

MY DAUGHTER!
DON'T WORRY, DR. LEE, I'LL—
YOU'LL DO NOTHING!
THAT YOU, BOSS? WITHOUT YOUR BADGE YOU ALL LOOK THE SAME! HA HA!
CLICK

UNCLE MATT?!
WHAT ARE YOU DOING?!
YOU'VE LOST CONTROL...!
NEPHEW! MY GOOD AND LOYAL KNIGHT!
I'VE BEEN ALL BUT ABANDONED, BUT YOU WILL STAY BY MY SIDE UNTIL THE VERY END!
GO, CHUCK! GET OUTTA HERE!

HEY, JERK IN THE GREEN BATHROBE! LET GO OF MY SISTER!
YOU?! YOU SHOULD HAVE ALREADY BEEN TAKEN CARE OF, BOY!

HOW ABOUT I TRY AGAIN?
VVVRRR...

TOSS
CHUCK!

K-RACK!
RGH!
RGH!
WHUMP!
SMACK!
RRRGH!
NEPHEW...?! YOU'RE SIDING WITH *THEM?!* OVER YOUR OWN *FLESH AND BLOOD?!*
CHUCK HERE IS SIDING WITH WHAT'S *RIGHT!*
BECAUSE WHAT *YOU'RE* DOING IS SO OBVIOUSLY *WRONG!*
NOT JUST WRONG. *EVIL.*

YOU'LL PAY FOR YOUR BETRAYAL, CHUCK RIGGS!
YOU'LL ALL PAY!
VVVFFF...
ZNNAAAPPPRRKTTT

HA! WILSON WAS RIGHT!
HE DOESN'T SMELL LIKE COTTON CANDY CLOUDS AT ALL.
HE SMELLS LIKE ASHES.
YES!
SUPERMAN... CAN FLY?!

HOW IS HE HOVERING IN THE AIR LIKE THAT?! IT'S NOT HUMANLY POSSIBLE!
HE'S SOME KINDA GHOST!
MONSTER!
DEMON!
FOR THE FIRST TIME IN A LONG, LONG WHILE, NORMAL PEOPLE LOOK AT ME WITH FEAR.
EXCEPT LOIS.
SHE'S THE SAME AS EVER. UTTERLY FEARLESS.
DEEP DOWN INSIDE, I KNEW FROM THE MOMENT I MET HER.
I KNEW LOIS COULD NEVER BE AFRAID OF ME, EVEN AFTER SHE LEARNED THE TRUTH.
THAT'S WHY I FELL IN LOVE WITH HER.
YOU ALL WANT TO KNOW HOW HE CAN FLY?!
HOW HE CAN SHOOT HEAT RAYS OUT OF HIS EYES?!
YOUR MOST BELOVED CITIZEN ISN'T A CITIZEN AT ALL!
GO ON, SUPERMAN! TELL THEM WHAT YOU REALLY ARE!

PEOPLE OF METROPOLIS... I...I...
I'M FROM ANOTHER PLACE.
I WAS BORN IN A DISTANT GALAXY, ON A PLANET CALLED KRYPTON. I CAME HERE AS AN INFANT.
BUT I AM STILL THE MAN YOU'VE ALWAYS KNOWN!
I'M STILL YOUR FELLOW CITIZEN!
YOU SEE NOW?! THE KLAN OF THE FIERY KROSS HAS ALWAYS PROTECTED AMERICA FROM FOREIGN THREATS!
AND SUPERMAN IS THE MOST FOREIGN OF THEM ALL!
GRAND SCORPION! TAKE DOWN THAT—THAT ALIEN!
SEND HIM BACK WHERE HE CAME FROM!
WHAT?! HOW MANY TIMES HAS SUPERMAN SAVED OUR CITY?!
AND YOU'RE GONNA TURN ON HIM JUST LIKE THAT?!
SAVE US, GRAND SCORPION!
PEOPLE! THIS IS SUPERMAN WE'RE TALKING ABOUT!
YOU HEAR THAT, ALIEN? ALL THE REAL ONE HUNDRED PERCENT AMERICANS WANT YOU EXTERMINATED!
AND I'VE GOT JUST THE WEAPON TO DO IT!
VVVFFF...

DIE, YOU ALIEN SCUM!
FFFWWWOOOSH!
GRF!
I'M OVERWHELMED BY THE SMELL OF ASH AND ROT AND... A DYING PLANET.
I FIGHT TO STAY CONSCIOUS.
UUUH...!
THAT WEAPON MUST BE POWERED BY DER GRÜNSTEIN! IT'S KILLING SUPERMAN!

THE ONLY THING THAT CAN STOP ITS RADIATION...
IS LEAD.
SUPERMAN! CATCH!
USE IT TO STOP HIS WEAPON!
THWAP!
GRAAA-
WHAT... ?!
KLINK!
VVVWWWEEE-!

KA
BOOOM!
STRENGTH FLOODS BACK INTO MY BODY.
IT FEELS LIKE DAWN.

GET HIM, SUPERMAN!
YEEEAH!

WHA...?!

WANNA KNOW HOW TO TELL US APART?
SMACK!
I'M THE ONE WITH THE AUTHORITY TO ARREST YOUR SORRY BEHIND!

IT'S OVER, GRAND SCORPION.
SURRENDER.

OH, IT'S OVER, BUT NOT THE WAY YOU THINK!
METROPOLIS MUST PAY!
WE ALL MUST PAY!
HA HA HA!
TICK TICK TICK TICK
TICK TICK TICK

TICK
TICK
TICK
TICK
TICK
TICK
TICK
TICK
TICK

TICK
TICK—
WOOOOO!
H-HOW DID YOU DO THAT?!
I'M NOT TOTALLY SURE. I'VE BEEN DISCOVERING A LOT ABOUT MYSELF LATELY.
KRK!
YOU REALLY ARE A FOOL, SUPERMAN! YOU HAVE SUCH POWER, EVEN I MUST CONCEDE THAT YOU ARE THE TRUE SUPERIOR RACE!
WHY FIGHT FOR A FAMILY OF CHING-CHONGS?
WHERE I'M FROM, WE TAKE CARE OF OUR OWN.
YOU'RE CALLING THE LEES "YOUR OWN"?
YES.
HA HA! YOU'VE BEEN BRAINWASHED BY CORRUPT NEWSPAPERS AND TEXTBOOKS, SUPERMAN!
THE LEES AREN'T "YOUR OWN"! YOU SHARE NO BLOOD WITH THEM! NO HISTORY! THERE IS LITERALLY NOTHING THAT BINDS YOU TOGETHER!
THAT HAS BEEN THE KLAN'S POINT ALL ALONG!
A NATION BOUND BY NOTHING CANNOT LAST!

BUT WE ARE BOUND TOGETHER.
THE LEES AND I...OUR FRIENDS AT THE DAILY PLANET AND THE UNITY HOUSE AND THE POLICE DEPARTMENT... EVERYONE DOWN THERE, REALLY...
WE ARE BOUND TOGETHER BY THE FUTURE.
WE ALL SHARE THE SAME TOMORROW.
THAT INCLUDES EVEN YOU, ONCE YOU'VE RENOUNCED YOUR HATE AND PAID FOR WHAT YOU'VE DONE.
I'D RATHER HAVE NO TOMORROW AT ALL!
HRK!
SLASH!
HAHA HA HA!
SUPERMAN!
HNNN...

!

THERE'S *ALWAYS* A TOMORROW.

LATER.
MS. LANE.
SUPERMAN.
I'VE GOT MY USUAL QUESTIONS. YOU FINALLY READY TO GIVE ME ANSWERS?

I AM. SOME OF THEM, ANYWAY.
ARE YOU A COFFEE DRINKER?

SUPERMAN CAN FLY! I DON'T KNOW IF I'LL EVER GET USED TO SEEING THAT!
YOU SAID IT.

THE GAME'S GONNA HAVE TO BE RESCHEDULED.
THAT DOESN'T MEAN **WE** CAN'T STILL PLAY! IT'D BE A PITY TO LET ALL THIS ***BEAUTIFUL SUNSHINE*** GO TO WASTE!
YOU ALL SHOULD FIND A FIELD THAT ISN'T SO TORN UP, THOUGH.

HEY, CHUCK! I'M GONNA GO INVITE THE ***GOTHAM KIDS*** TO JOIN US FOR A PICKUP. WANNA COME ALONG?
GO ON, SON. GO WITH YOUR ***FRIENDS.*** I'LL BE ALL RIGHT.
WE'LL BE ALL RIGHT.

ROBERTA! ***CATCH!*** I SAW HOW YOU THREW THAT METAL BALL TO SUPERMAN!
YOU'RE ***PITCHING!***

Daily Planet

SUPERMAN: IMMIGRANT FROM KRYPTON, CITIZEN OF METROPOLIS

His "S" Is an Ancient Symbol for Hope

HI, MR. KENT!

ROBERTA LEE! NICE TO SEE YOU!

HOW'S THE REST OF THE FAMILY?

HMMM...
MS. LANE? I DON'T MEAN TO BOTHER YOU...
ROBERTA! WHAT A LOVELY SURPRISE!

I CAME TO GIVE THIS PEN BACK TO YOU. IT'S TOO EXPENSIVE. I CAN'T ACCEPT IT.
NONSENSE!
YOU'RE GOING TO NEED IT FOR YOUR NEW JOB.

I WAS SERIOUS ABOUT THAT CUB REPORTER POSITION.
REALLY...?!

BUT STILL...IT HAS YOUR INITIALS ON IT. YOU SHOULD HAVE IT.
YOU KNOW I ALWAYS DO MY HOMEWORK, DON'T YOU?
WHEN I WROTE THAT ARTICLE ABOUT WHAT HAPPENED TO YOUR FAMILY, I RESEARCHED YOUR FATHER, YOUR MOTHER, YOUR BROTHER—

—AND YOU, LAN-SHIN LEE.

MY NAME IS LAN-SHIN LEE.
I'M A CUB REPORTER FOR THE DAILY PLANET.
I'VE WORKED HARD TO MAKE METROPOLIS—THE CITY OF TOMORROW—MY HOME.
JUST LIKE SUPERMAN.
THE END.

THE END

SUPERMAN AND ME
By Gene Luen Yang

Figure 1. Superman as he appeared in the Fleischer Studios cartoons of the 1940s.

In 1946, Superman took down a gang of robed, hooded white supremacists. He did it over sixteen episodes of *The Adventures of Superman*, America's most popular radio show at the time. The plot went something like this: A Chinese American family moves to Metropolis. The Clan of the Fiery Cross, fictional stand-ins for the real-life Ku Klux Klan, burns a tall wooden cross on the family's lawn. Superman leaps to the family's defense.

When I first heard about it, I thought, "A Chinese American family? Neat!" I've watched and read Superman stories since I was little. I wasn't used to finding characters in them who looked like me.

Figure 2. Portrait of an African American Union soldier and his family, taken between 1863 and 1865. Courtesy of the Library of Congress, LC-DIG-ppmsca-36454.

In January of 1865, when the bloody Civil War was nearing its end, the federal government of the United States passed the Thirteenth Amendment, which abolished slavery except as a way to punish crime.

Later that same year, a group of men gathered together in Tennessee for the very first meeting of the Ku Klux Klan. These men believed in white supremacy, the idea that people from Western and Northern Europe are just plain better than all other kinds of people. They feared that the newly freed black slaves would ask for equal rights and equal treatment.

The Klan terrorized African Americans and their white allies not just in Tennessee, but all across the South. They issued threats, burned down churches, and murdered countless people.

I can't remember when I first discovered Superman. Was it the classic 1978 movie starring Christopher Reeve? Or the old *Super Friends* cartoon? Or the Superman puzzle book I bought at a school book fair in the first grade?

I don't know for sure. He seems to have always been there.

I liked his powers, of course, but I loved his costume. The emblem on his chest looked like a badge, or maybe a shield. It told everybody that he was Superman, and that was awesome.

In 1865, white supremacists in California read newspaper articles about the Ku Klux Klan in the South. They felt inspired. Few African Americans lived on the West Coast, but plenty of Chinese did.

People who looked like me first began coming to America in large numbers at the beginning of the 1800s. By the time the Civil War ended, Chinese made up ten percent of California's population, and more were coming.

The federal government was already making noise about granting African Americans the right to vote. If they did the same for Chinese immigrants, what would become of white supremacy in the West?

In 1868, a missive appeared in the San Francisco Bay Area calling the Ku Klux Klan to "Action! Action! Action!" Soon after, Klansmen started terrorizing Chinese immigrants and their white allies not just in California, but up and down the West Coast. They issued threats, burned down churches, and murdered countless people.

The terrorism in the West was never as widespread nor as organized as the terrorism in the South, but it was still terrifying. The largest mass lynching in California's history happened in Los Angeles Chinatown in 1871. A mob rampaged through a Chinatown street known as Negro Alley. Although the mob did not explicitly claim to be the Klan, they definitely acted Klan-like. They hanged to death between seventeen and twenty Chinese men and boys.

I've never had a run-in with the Ku Klux Klan. The racism I encountered as a kid wasn't nearly as dramatic as a fiery cross. It was quiet and subtle.

In the seventh grade, I wrote a story about Cobra Commander's death. Cobra Commander is the archenemy of G.I. Joe, a team of superhero soldiers who ruled after-school cartoons in the 1980s.

Mr. Stevens, my teacher, liked my story so much that he read it to the whole class. He ended in his most ominous voice, "As Cobra Commander breathed his last, he hissed, 'G.I. Joe has won!'"

The other students clapped. I tried to keep my smile as humble as possible.

"G.I. Joe," one of my classmates said to me. "Cool story."

We'll call him Danny. Danny was broad-shouldered, hazel-eyed, and athletic. He wore clothes that you saw on billboards. And he never tied his shoes, which everybody thought was awesome.

He gave me a thumbs-up. My smile stopped being humble.

Later in P.E., I saw Danny standing on the soccer field. He'd actually talked to me, I thought. I ought to return the favor.

Figure 3. My little brother and me in our awesome 1980s outfits. Used with permission.

I walked up to him. "Hey, Danny," I said.

"Hey," he said. "G.I. Joe. Cool story, man! High five!"

He put his hand up.

As soon as I reached for it, he pulled back.

"I'm not touching no..." Then Danny said a word that rhymes with "stink."

I watched his shoelaces drag along the grass as he walked away.

After the Civil War, white supremacist politicians in the South began enacting Black Codes, laws that made sure African Americans would remain second-class citizens. Although the Fifteenth Amendment granted African American men the right to vote, the codes kept them out of the voting booth. They also kept them out

Figure 4. Portrait of a Chinese American family, taken between 1898 and 1905. Courtesy of the Library of Congress, LC-DIG-ppmsca-17885.

of white neighborhoods, schools, churches, and even restrooms. The codes became popularly known as Jim Crow laws.

White supremacists in the West came up with an even more clever tactic. They saw that the federal government no longer tolerated slavery, so they began to argue that Chinese immigrants were actually slaves. They pointed out that the Chinese worked in terrible, slave-like conditions. If America really wanted to get rid of slavery, they said, the country had to close its borders to the Chinese.

Their argument was ridiculous. Chinese immigrants did live unquestionably difficult lives. They were often the victims of brutal, unfair contracts, and they couldn't fight back because their testimony wasn't recognized in American courts.

But as bad as things were, they weren't slaves. Nobody could sell off their loved ones at a moment's notice.

Even so, the tactic worked. In 1882, America passed the Chinese Exclusion Act, effectively ending all legal immigration from China to the United States.

By the end of the 1800s, with Jim Crow laws and the Chinese Exclusion Act in place, the Ku Klux Klan no longer felt threatened by African Americans in the South or Chinese immigrants in the West. People stopped joining, and their membership shrank.

Shortly after the incident with Danny, I started pestering my mom to take me to the local mall. One Saturday afternoon, she finally did. I made a beeline for a store called Aca Joe that sold clothes you saw on billboards.

I picked out a bright white sweatshirt with the store's logo on the chest, the letters ACA stenciled in an oval. It looked like a badge, or maybe a shield.

I silently hoped that it would protect me from that word that rhymes with "stink."

It did not.

In 1915, a movie called *The Birth of a Nation* opened in theaters all across America. It portrays the Ku Klux Klan as a team of white supremacist "heroes" who hide their identities underneath robes and hoods while "defending" the country against the "threat" of the newly freed slaves. In one scene, Klansmen burn a tall wooden cross, a fiery symbol of their hatred. The real-life Klan had never done this before.

The movie was a hit. Audiences flocked to see it. Companies sold Klan-themed merchandise like hats and aprons. Fans hosted Klan-themed parties and invited their friends to come dressed up as Klansmen. *The Birth of a Nation* made between $50 and $100 million, making it the first-ever blockbuster movie. Even President Woodrow Wilson was a fan. After watching the film at a special screening at the White House, he described it admiringly as "writing history with lightning."

Within a few months, the Ku Klux Klan was back in business. And this time, they *were* a business. They hired a publicity agency to help them make as much money as possible.

One of their strategies was to expand their circle of hate to include more kinds of people. The new Klan didn't just hate African Americans and Chinese immigrants, they also hated Mexicans, Middle Easterners, Japanese, and Filipinos, as well as Roman Catholics and Jews from Eastern and Southern Europe.

Although they continued the Klan tradition of violence, the second Klan started hosting family-friendly events like picnics and parades to attract new members. Taking a cue from the movie, they burned tall wooden crosses at their events.

The second Ku Klux Klan was a hit. At its peak, it had several million dues-paying members.

Superman first appeared in 1938, in the very first issue of a comic book series called *Action Comics*. The hero was very different from how he is now. The S emblem on his chest hadn't yet evolved into its familiar diamond shape. He worked at a newspaper called the *Daily Star*, not the *Daily Planet*. Lois Lane was in the office, but Jimmy Olsen and Perry White were nowhere to be seen.

His powers were different, too. He was super-strong and super-fast, but he couldn't fly. He could only leap. He couldn't shoot heat rays out of his eyes or blow freeze breath from his mouth, either. Those would come later.

Superman was created by two teenagers in Cleveland, Ohio, named Jerry Siegel and Joe Shuster. They were

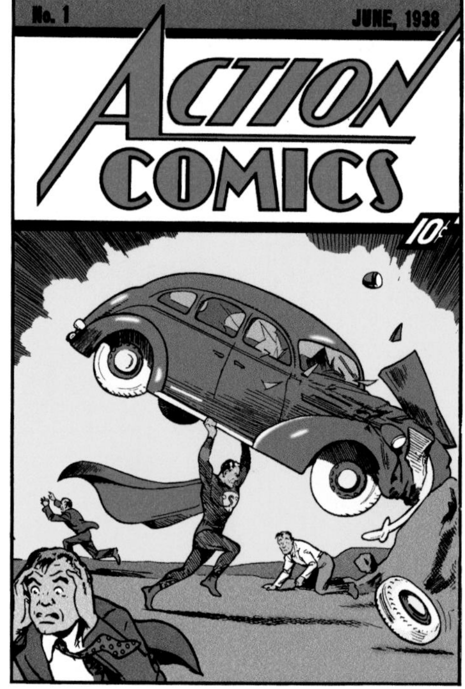

Figure 5. *Action Comics* #1, cover art by Joe Shuster.

both sons of Jewish immigrants. As white supremacist ideas grew stronger and stronger in Europe, hatred for Jews grew worse and worse. Jerry and Joe's families worried that things would turn violent, so they escaped to America.

To fit in better, both families changed their last names. The Siegels were originally the Segalovichs and the Shusters were the Shusterowichs. Unfortunately, the name change did not protect them from hate. When Jerry and Joe were growing up in Cleveland, it wasn't uncommon for job ads in the local newspaper to say, "No Jews Need Apply."

Often, Jews could only find work in the roughest parts of town. Jerry's dad ran a secondhand clothing store in just such a neighborhood. When Jerry was 17 years old, someone tried to rob the store. Jerry's dad suffered a heart attack and died.

Jerry and his friend Joe loved stories about aliens, space men, and other planets. They loved them so much that they created their own fanzine called *Science Fiction*.

In the third issue of *Science Fiction*, published in 1933, Jerry and Joe wrote and drew a story titled

Figure 6. Joe Shuster and Jerry Siegel, creators of Superman, with M.C. Gaines.

"The Reign of the Superman," about a man who gets mind-control powers, turns evil, and tries to destroy the world by spreading hateful thoughts. In the end, a do-gooder reporter confronts this evil "Superman" to save the day.

In the five years between *Science Fiction* #3 and *Action Comics* #1, Jerry and Joe came up with several game-changing ideas.

First, they decided to make Superman good. Instead of having mind-control powers like a mad scientist, they made him strong and fast, like a pulp magazine hero.

Second, they dressed him up like a circus strongman. Circuses were very popular back then. Performers wore colorful, skin-tight costumes so that audience members in the back row could still see them.

Finally, Jerry and Joe made Superman an alien from another planet. He would be an immigrant, like their parents, and he would hide his identity underneath a red tie, a white shirt, a blue jacket, and a pair of glasses. He even had another name to fit in better: Clark Kent.

Superman was a hit. Readers flocked to buy his comics. Demand for Superman merchandise was so intense that his publisher had to set up Superman Inc., a subsidiary dedicated to licensing the hero's likeness. Soon, kids all across America were playing with Superman paper dolls, puzzles, and paint sets.

Then on Monday, February 12, 1940, Superman made his way to radio, America's most popular entertainment medium at the time.

It was on the radio that Superman would make one of his most important contributions to America.

By the end of the 1930s, war had broken out in Europe and Asia. Jerry and Joe's parents' worst nightmares came true. German white supremacists called Nazis began to systematically arrest and murder the Jews in their country.

At first, America tried to stay neutral.

Then on December 7, 1941, the Empire of Japan, an ally of Nazi Germany, attacked an American naval base at Pearl Harbor in Honolulu, Hawaii. More than two thousand Americans were killed.

Japan, Germany, and Italy had formed an alliance known as the Axis. Within days, President Franklin D. Roosevelt declared war on all three Axis powers. America had officially entered World War II.

Back then, the United States army observed Jim Crow by separating American soldiers into regiments by race. The army's nonwhite regiments were not as well equipped nor as well supported as the white regiments. Nonwhite soldiers were often passed over for promotions to leadership positions.

This hypocrisy infuriated many Americans. In January of 1942, a young African American named James G. Thompson wrote a letter to the *Pittsburgh Courier*. In it, he expresses how much he wants to serve his country and help America defeat the "forces of evil." But he also asks, "Should I sacrifice my life to live half American?"

He ends his letter by challenging America to fight for two victories: a victory against the Axis powers abroad and a victory against inequality at home.

A double victory.

African Americans enlisted in record numbers, far more than for the first World War. Other nonwhite Americans did, too. They fought in the hopes of James G. Thompson's double victory.

The attack on Pearl Harbor changed things for Chinese Americans in an unexpected way. Almost overnight, our public image flipped.

DC Comics, the publisher of this graphic novel, is named after *Detective Comics*, the company's longest-running title. That's what the letters DC stand for: Detective Comics.

The very first issue of *Detective Comics* came out in 1937, four years before America entered the war. The cover shows a drawing of a Chinese villain with slanted, demonic eyes and an evil frown. Before Pearl Harbor, this was how many Americans thought of the Chinese: sneaky, criminal, and threatening. If you wanted to buy something illegal, you would go to the neighborhood where all the Chinese people lived.

After Pearl Harbor, America realized that China was its greatest ally against Japan. Suddenly, Chinese Americans weren't sneaky, criminal, and threatening anymore. We became hardworking, loyal, and brave.

Figure 7. President Roosevelt signs a declaration of war against Japan. Courtesy of the Library of Congress, LC-USZ62-15185.

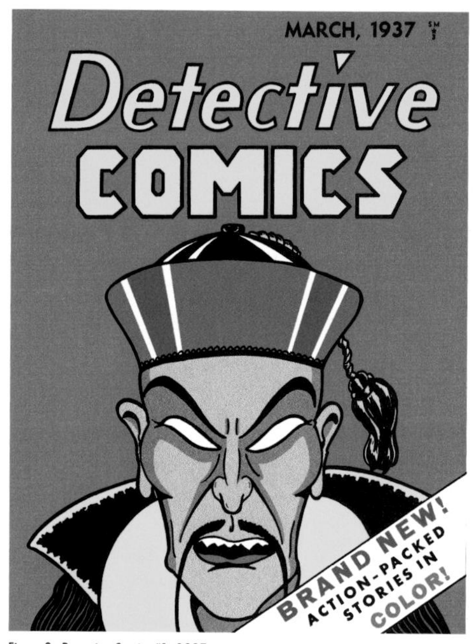

Figure 8. *Detective Comics* #1, 1937.

Unlike African American and Japanese American soldiers, some Chinese American soldiers were even allowed to integrate into white regiments.

On December 21, 1941, *Time* magazine published

an issue about Pearl Harbor. The cover shows a drawing of Yamamoto Isoroku, the Japanese admiral who had masterminded the attack. The artist drew Admiral Yamamoto with slanted, demonic eyes and an evil frown.

The stereotypes that were once applied to the Chinese had been refocused solely on the Japanese.

That same issue of *Time* has an article titled, "How to tell our friends from the Japs." It lists instructions to figure out if a person is Chinese or Japanese. After decades of being villains, the Chinese in America were now friends.

In February of 1942, an executive order signed by President Roosevelt forced Japanese Americans out of their homes and into internment camps until the war's end. It seemed like a reasonable strategy for dealing with a sneaky, criminal, and threatening population.

People of German and Italian descent were also interned, albeit on a much smaller scale, though the vast majority were not citizens. Sixty-two percent of the internees in the Japanese camps were citizens of the United States.

The Adventures of Superman radio show starred Clayton "Bud" Collyer, one of the most in-demand voice actors of the 1930s and '40s. With his tall frame and thin mustache, he didn't look much like Clark Kent, but because of his uncanny ability to switch from nerdy newspaper reporter to superhero, Collyer became the first actor to ever play Superman.

The show was a hit. After just two months of episodes, it topped the charts as the highest-rated kids' program in America. Millions of listeners tuned in three times a week, and their hunger for stories encouraged the writers to quickly develop their hero and his world. The show introduced many important pieces of the Superman mythos, including the *Daily Planet*, Perry White, and Kryptonite. Even Superman's powers evolved. He switched from leaping to flying for the first time on his radio show.

During World War II, Superman faced off against Nazi villains like Der Teufel, the Scarlet Widow, and the Atom Man.

Superman spent the war years fighting hate.

On May 8, 1945, Nazi Germany surrendered. Japan surrendered three months later on September 2. America and our allies had won.

The year before, on June 22, 1944, President Roosevelt had signed the G.I. Bill into law. The bill offered the men and women who had served so valiantly in World War II a number of benefits, including money for college and loans to buy homes and start businesses.

Veterans returned home full of hope. This was especially true of nonwhite veterans since the G.I. Bill did not contain any language that excluded them because of their race. After years of sacrifice, the double victory seemed to finally be within reach.

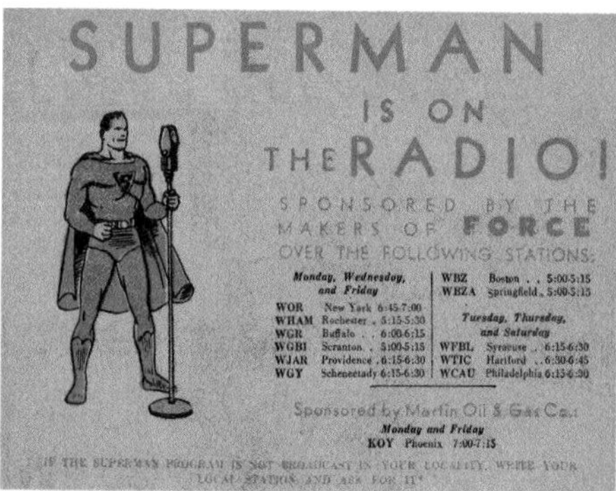

Figure 9. Ad for *The Adventures of Superman* radio show.

By this time, *The Adventures of Superman* was more popular than ever, with four million listeners per episode, but it needed a new direction. Now that the Nazis had been defeated in real life, Superman couldn't keep fighting them in fiction.

But who was a threat to peace in postwar America?

Not everyone looked forward to the possibility of a double victory. On the evening of May 9, 1946, a doctor named Samuel Green led a group of men up Stone Mountain, near Atlanta, Georgia. Green was a grand dragon of the Ku Klux Klan.

As grand dragon, Green had watched the second Klan collapse before the war. Many Klansmen left once they realized the entire operation was just a money-making scheme. Others left after their leaders' criminal behavior came to light. One Klan leader had been convicted of murdering his secretary. Another was in prison for murdering a rival. Still others were arrested for bribery and theft.

Samuel Green longed for a Klan revival. That night on Stone Mountain, he and his followers built a tall wooden cross and set it on fire. They announced a brand-new era of hate.

As Green had hoped, newspapers all over the nation covered the ceremony. *Life* magazine even published a three-page photo spread. Although the text called the Klansmen bigots, the gorgeously shot photos showed well-dressed, clean-cut men gathered around a fiery cross that shone brightly against a dark sky.

The Ku Klux Klan was about to get back on its feet.

The Klan's original revival had been inspired by a movie about men in white robes.

Its next revival would be stifled by a radio show about a man in a red cape.

No one is sure who first came up with the idea. Stetson Kennedy, an intrepid anti-Klan reporter, said he had brought the idea to the radio show's staff. Kenyon and Eckhardt, an advertising agency that worked with the show, said the idea was actually theirs.

Bob Maxwell, the head of Superman Inc., claimed he had to convince Kenyon and Eckhardt to get on board. He certainly had reason for wanting his company's premier superhero to take on the Klan. As a Jewish American, Maxwell recoiled in horror when he read about what white supremacists had done to Jewish people in Europe. He felt a duty to fight bigotry however he could.

To avoid getting sued by an organization that was legally recognized by several states, the show's writers created a stand-in organization called the Clan of the Fiery Cross. There was no mistaking their intention, though. The fictional villains had the same costumes, rituals, and beliefs as the real-life Ku Klux Klan.

Maxwell read through 25 different scripts before landing on the right one. There were plenty of risks, so he wanted to be careful. What if the story was too preachy? Or too scary? Superman might alienate his young fans.

Figure 10. Captain Barnes and Captain John C. Young, taken in 1944. Used with permission.

Figure 11. This photo of Arthur Hebert of the 1st Marine Division was taken in 1943. His father was lynched by the Ku Klux Klan the same year he was drafted. Used with permission.

Even worse, what if a listener only tuned in to a part of an episode and left with the impression that Superman actually condoned bigotry? The script had to get things just right.

On June 10, 1946, the first episode of the 16-part "The Clan of the Fiery Cross" story line aired. For the next several weeks, listeners all across America huddled around their radios to listen as young Tommy Lee, his father Dr. Lee, and his unnamed mother and sister moved into Metropolis and ran afoul of a group of violent bigots. They cheered when Superman leapt to the family's defense.

The story line had its detractors. Klan supporters in Atlanta called for a boycott of the show's sponsors. Bob Maxwell even received death threats from the New Jersey Klan.

Most people, though, loved it. *The Adventures of Superman* received awards from the United Parents Association and the Boys Clubs of America. *Newsweek* magazine called it "the first children's program to develop a social consciousness." Listenership soared.

Some believe that Superman's radio defeat of the Clan of the Fiery Cross led to the real-life Klan's public image downfall. After being portrayed as bumbling, hateful rubes on a children's show, the Ku Klux Klan would never again command the same level of respect it had once enjoyed.

After World War II, many Chinese American veterans did what the Lee family did in "The Clan of the Fiery Cross." With help from the G.I. Bill, they moved out of the nation's Chinatowns and into the suburbs.

They were often met with hostility. Once they got to their new neighborhoods, some were threatened. Others had garbage thrown on their lawns. Some chose to move in the middle of the night to avoid trouble.

Even so, in part because of the public image shift that had happened after Pearl Harbor, Chinese Americans were able to make the move.

Not all nonwhite Americans were as lucky. Black veterans had a much harder time accessing the G.I. Bill's benefits, despite the bill not having any language about race. In the South, where most African Americans lived, the federal government handed over the bill's administration to racist local officials. Many black veterans were denied the home loans they had rightfully earned, so they were unable to make the same move the Chinese Americans had made.

Japanese Americans also faced hardships. Even after they were released from the internment camps, most could not recover the homes and businesses that had been taken from them. Their own government had erased their pre-war lives.

"The Clan of the Fiery Cross is made up of intolerant bigots," Clark Kent tells Jimmy Olsen in the "Clan" story line's third episode. "They don't judge a man in the decent American way by his own qualities, they judge him by what church he goes to, and by the color of his skin.

"Intolerance is a filthy weed," he continues. "The only way to get rid of it is by hunting out the roots and pulling them out of the ground!"

Superman was leading us to a bright new tomorrow. Unfortunately, postwar America didn't follow him all the way. We left the double victory incomplete.

My mother was born in China in 1945, a year before the end of World War II. During the first years of her life, her family moved from one city to the next, trying their best to escape violence and starvation. They eventually made it to Hong Kong and then Taiwan.

After graduating from a Taiwanese college, my mother came to the United States. She met my father, who had also come from Taiwan. The two of them went on to earn master's degrees despite not having completely mastered English. They courageously faced down racism and other indignities and went on to build a life for themselves and their family.

My parents were able to achieve all that they have not only because they worked hard (and believe me, they worked hard), but also because they immigrated over two decades after the Lees first moved to Metropolis, to an America that had not given up the struggle for a true double victory.

Figure 12. My mother around the time she came to America. Used with premission.

Figure 13. My father and his friend Dave when they were college students. Used with permission.

We are still in the midst of that struggle.

After my father arrived in America and before he met my mom, he was terribly lonely. He lived in a boarding house with other students. One of them was named Dave. Dave had dark brown hair and Clark Kent glasses, and he'd grown up in a town that was driving distance from campus.

Dave must have sensed that my father needed a friend. Despite the language barrier, Dave began talking with my father. First one conversation, then another. On holidays when the house cleared out, Dave invited my father to go with him to his parents' home. Dave's parents and siblings welcomed my father with open arms, and they shared many meals together.

"I felt a lot less lonesome during the holidays," my father says. "I'm grateful for that warm friendship."

Fifty years have passed. My father and Dave each found wives, raised families, started and then ended careers. They are friends to this day.

When I think about what the future ought to be like, I don't think about my junior high classmate with the untied shoes. I think about the friendship between my dad and Dave.

Superman is one of our nation's—and the world's—most enduring icons. He seems to have always been there, and he's not going away anytime soon. Ever since defending a Chinese American family in 1946, he's stood for tolerance, justice, and hope.

Even today, the immigrant from Krypton challenges us to follow his example more fully and more perfectly.

We have to meet his challenge.

After all, though our yesterdays may be different, we all share the same tomorrow.

Gene Luen Yang

August 2019

Bibliography

Superman Versus the Ku Klux Klan: The True Story of How the Iconic Superhero Battled the Men of Hate by Richard Bowers (National Geographic Society, 2012)

The Chinese in America: A Narrative History by Iris Chang (Penguin Books, 2004)

The Second Coming of the KKK: The Ku Klux Klan of the 1920s and the American Political Tradition by Linda Gordon (Liveright, 2017)

When Affirmative Action Was White: An Untold History of Racial Inequality in Twentieth-Century America by Ira Katznelson (W. W. Norton & Company, 2006)

Stamped from the Beginning: The Definitive History of Racist Ideas in America by Ibram X. Kendi (Bold Type Books, 2017)

Freakonomics: A Rogue Economist Explores the Hidden Side of Everything by Steven D. Levitt and Stephen J. Dubner (William Morrow Paperbacks, 2009)

Rising Out of Hatred: The Awakening of a Former White Nationalist by Eli Saslow (Doubleday, 2018)

Freedom's Frontier: California and the Struggle over Unfree Labor, Emancipation, and Reconstruction by Stacey L. Smith (The University of North Carolina Press, 2013)

"California's first #resistance," by Kevin Waite (*Los Angeles Times*, August 5, 2018)

Superman: The Unauthorized Biography by Glen Weldon (Wiley, 2013)

Gene Luen Yang writes, and sometimes draws, comic books and graphic novels. As the Library of Congress's fifth National Ambassador for Young People's Literature, he advocates for the importance of reading, especially reading diversely. *American Born Chinese*, his first graphic novel from First Second Books, was a National Book Award finalist, as well as the winner of the Printz Award and an Eisner Award. His companion graphic novel project *Boxers* and *Saints* won the L.A. Times Book Prize and was a National Book Award finalist. His other works include *Secret Coders* (with Mike Holmes), *The Shadow Hero* (with Sonny Liew), *Superman* from DC Comics (with various artists), and the *Avatar: The Last Airbender* series from Dark Horse Comics (with Gurihiru). In 2016, he was named a MacArthur Foundation Fellow. His most recent books are *Dragon Hoops* from First Second Books and *Superman Smashes the Klan* from DC Comics.

Gurihiru is a team name for Chifuyu Sasaki (pencils and inks) and Naoko Kawano (colors). They are freelance illustrators living in Saitama, Japan. While working on comic books published in the U.S., such as *The Unstoppable Wasp* (Marvel) and the *Avatar: The Last Airbender* graphic novel series (Dark Horse Comics) they also work on many other projects in Japan including video games, animation character designs, and book illustrations.